CW01507454

# WALDMEER

A SPIRITUAL FICTION SERIES

WALDMEER SERIES
BOOK 1

## DONNA GODDARD

Waldmeer is based on the idyllic coastal village of Lorne, Victoria. Eraldus is based on the inner-city suburb of Northcote, Australia.

# CONTENTS

## HEALING

## BODY

## BEING SAVED

## NEW BEGINNING

PART II
## IN ERALDUS
The Dividing Line

## THE CITY

## TRUST

## LANEWAYS

## MIR STREET

## MEN

## BLISS

## CHANGE

## HAPPY MOMENTS

# PART I
# IN WALDMEER

SPIRIT ON EARTH

# THE GARDEN

# CHAPTER 1
# ONE WHO SPEAKS

I*n the spirit world of a garden on Earth:*
    The gardener walked into their lives bright and sharp. A ready smile covered her need. She came from a house with walls that echoed loneliness. On the very first day, her eyes were drawn to the little flower in the corner of the garden. Its beauty was in its simplicity. The gardener's jealousy was already born. She watched it every day. It moved to the breeze and reached for the sunshine. The flower did not complain about the dark, the wind, or the cold. Its roots had strength unseen.

The little flower was called Amira. Farkas, the garden spirit, guarded her. He loved Amira most of all the garden residents. However, he was wounded. He had lived many lives and carried the damage inside himself. He often went away, and they would not see him for long periods. Sometimes, he would sit near Amira and remember things he rarely let himself remember. He would rest there until the wind called him away again.

The gardener watched it all, and her loathing grew darker.

*How can the little flower have such a hold over the garden spirit's heart?* she thought.

One morning, before the rising light had given its blessing to the day, the gardener, sick with her longing, left her bed and killed the little flower.

*Now, Farkas will learn to love me,* she thought. *He will come to look at me and feel alive. He will protect me instead of the pathetic, dead flower.*

When Farkas next returned, he went to greet Amira. He had missed his sweet friend. His eyes filled with rage when he saw that his little love was gone. He knew instantly what had happened and stormed to the gardener with fire and death in his breath. The gardener was frightened.

"I only wanted you to love me," she said.

"You cannot kill another being and then claim their spirit as your own," he spat at her. "I despise you."

Still, he let her stay in the garden. She reminded him that he hated life. He wanted to hate life.

Despite Farkas's disgust for her, the gardener still longed for him. She waited for his return, but the absences became longer until he barely returned at all. When he did, he gave her nothing of his essence. The garden became a soulless place. It had no nourishment. One day, the gardener realised that if she stayed any longer, she too would be consumed by the slow death. And so, she left. She did not say goodbye. She did not wish to prolong the pain.

THE GARDEN WAS VERY STILL. A gentle breeze moved through the silent trees. It stirred the long, dry grass. A lone bird landed on a high branch. Surprisingly, it stayed there. Farkas was far away, but he sensed that something had changed. He could feel a quickening movement in his soul. He returned to the garden and looked around. Not much was alive.

Nevertheless, there was a subtle, sweet scent that had not been there before. In the place where the little flower had once lived, a tiny seed had sprouted and was holding onto earth and air with all its might. It was willing itself to grow into a strong and beautiful flower again. It looked so fragile. Fragility is the mask of mastery.

"I will stay here," Farkas called to the distant wind. "The garden needs me."

## CHAPTER 2
## THE GUILTLESS GARDEN

I n the inter-dimensional Garden of Garourinn in the North Country:

The gardener, Verloren, left in despair. Leaving was painful, but staying would have been worse. She went with nothing more than she had arrived with—except for one thing: guilt. She carried the guilt of murder and, just as heavy, the guilt of wanting to consume another being. After several weeks of travel, which seemed to be getting nowhere, she remembered a bedtime story her grandfather told her as a small child.

*Verloren, when you are weary, go to the Garden of Garourinn. It is in the North Country, where the winters are long and cold. You will find the Head Gardener there if you are so fortunate to be graced by his presence.*

It was the first clear idea that Verloren had had in a long time.

*Go quickly, girl,* she thought she heard her grandfather add. *The season has not yet turned, and you will be able to cross*

*to the North Country. If you wait any longer, the pass will freeze,*
*and you will indeed wait a long time until it is clear again.*

She set off immediately, feeling that no other option was
any less arduous. While travelling, she pondered with
surprise and relief that her grandfather's voice seemed to
hold no reproach.

*Perhaps,* she thought, *he doesn't know what I have done.*

She pushed the thought out of her mind, being sure it
was the case. Just as her grandfather said, the pass was not
yet frozen. With considerable effort, often having to retrace
her steps from wrong turns, she made it to the other side,
tired but unharmed. She glanced back at the pass and
realised she only had about one week before it would be
completely frozen. She needed to find the Garden of
Garourinn, procure an audience with the Head Gardener,
and then cross back over the pass before winter claimed the
land as its own.

The days went by. Not only could she not find
Garourinn, but everyone she asked gave conflicting advice.
Some said it was a myth, and she was wasting her time.
Some said it was high in the mountain but near impossible
to find. Some said they had just visited the garden that day,
and it was only up the road a little. She quickly followed the
directions, but there was no garden, and no one in that area
seemed to know of its existence.

The last day was upon her, and she had to make her way
back to the pass before it closed. She had a heavy heart. Her
mission had failed, and she had nothing to return to that was
worth living for. Perhaps it would be better to walk so slowly
that the pass did freeze, and then she could quietly go to
sleep in the cold and not wake up. Her slowing pace

suggested that this was the solution she had settled on. Verloren was startled by a sudden voice.

*Don't be foolish, girl,* said her grandfather. *Do you think that going to sleep will end your pain? It will not. Climb the next hill on your left, and you will find Garourinn.*

Wide awake and with hope in her heart, Verloren reached the crest of the hill. The view stole her breath.

*Perhaps I have already died,* she thought.

She seemed alive, so she walked down into the green valley, starkly contrasting the surrounding mountains of white, rocky ice. There were trees, grassy meadows, and little homes. Everything looked peaceful. The sun was somehow shining warmly on this valley only. The massive walls of cold mountain were forbidding, yet they acted as a protection for the valley without infringing on its microcosm.

Stopping at one of the little cottages because the door was ajar, Verloren entered and felt immediately at home. A fire was sharing soft, comforting light with the room. She realised that she was freezing, wet, and starving. There were clean, dry clothes on a chair. They seemed to belong to her, although they were much simpler than her typical taste in fashion. She gratefully took off her wet clothes and pulled the new ones on. Strangely, she had never felt so beautiful in any clothing she had ever bought.

Warm bread, creamy butter, fragrant cheese, and slices of red apple were on the table. A sweet lemon and orange drink was more delicious than anything Verloren had ever tasted. Feeling safe and content, she lay on the welcoming bed and instantly fell deeply asleep. She did not have a worry in the world and could not even recall why anyone could possibly be worried about anything.

The morning light made dancing patterns on the floor.

Verloren woke and suddenly remembered her quest. Having found the Garden of Garourinn, she must now find the Head Gardener. She recalled that there were things she wanted, and this was her chance to get them. The memory quickened her pulse.

Not seeing anyone to ask directions, she hastily walked back to the top of the hill to get a better view. She turned to the pass and saw that it had almost frozen over. On turning back to Garourinn, she saw, to her horror, that the garden valley was there no more. There was a sudden, panicked emptiness in her stomach, worse than before she found Garourinn.

*Hurry, Verloren,* the icy wind said as it swirled around her. *You have no more time. Run to the pass and cross now. You will not find Garourinn here again.*

Verloren ran to the pass, managed to cross it, and, on reaching the other side, fell to the ground in a sheltered place. She slept, exhausted and troubled. The following day, still utterly exhausted and unable to move, she tried to make sense of her journey.

*What a complete failure,* she thought. *I did not get to see the Head Gardener. I am no better off than when I started. All I had was one strange moment of peace that vanished as quickly as it came, as if to taunt me with the reality of my own existence.*

The hours passed as she walked, but the bleakness did not. It grew denser.

*Perhaps my grandfather will talk to me again,* she thought.

Presently, his gentle voice floated into the recesses of her mind, moving in and then vanishing as soon as she concentrated on it.

*If I relax,* she thought, *I may hear him better.*

The voice became more audible, and Verloren realised it was not her grandfather's.

"I am the one you sought," said the voice. "I am the Head Gardener. I am sorry that you could not see me this time. You are not ready. You did well. You found the Garden of Garourinn, if but for an instant. The healing you received there will help you to become lighter, and you will be able to tolerate the frequency of Garourinn for more extended periods before it disappears. Garourinn is my home. It is yours too. You will need to visit it many more times before you will be able to see me. Now that you have made the treacherous journey once, it will not be necessary for you to make it in person again. Instead, try to find it in your sleep. Each visit will strengthen you.
Let me leave you with these thoughts. You, like most Earth people, carry much self-loathing and guilt. You have done many bad things, many more than you currently admit to yourself, but that is alright because it is the same for almost everyone on Earth. Garourinn is the guiltless garden. Those who visit start to see their real form. They realise that they are, indeed, whole and beautiful. Seen as they are, all sense of guilt vanishes. Nothing exists except this truth in Garourinn. It is very pure and has tremendous healing power. Those who visit regularly bring that power back into their worlds. You see, Verloren, we strengthen in ourselves what we give to others. By the way, I know your grandfather well. He has been here many times, but these days, he mostly visits other lands."

# CHAPTER 3
# DON'T COME BACK

I n the spirit world of the Waldmeer garden:

Farkas tried to keep the little flower alive, but it was not going well. He wanted to settle into life in the garden, but was restless and distracted.

"I am not feeling well," said the little flower, Amira, softly one evening.

"You are so strong," said Farkas, looking worried.

"Make yourself well again," he commanded as if such a thing could be commanded.

"When I am a flower," Amira explained, "I rely on those who care for me. I cannot change that. I think you should go to the Homeland for a while. It is autumn here, and we will all survive without you for the coming months."

*In the inter-dimensional Homeland:*

When Farkas arrived at the Homeland, he was sent to the Vastandamine Forest and told to rest there. He went, but he could not rest. He knew, all too well, the talent of this forest. It would bring into one's experience whatever most needed healing. No one ever wanted to go there, yet everyone knew its benefit.

Sure enough, before long, he had a visitor. It was his last Earth father. The likeness was uncomfortably apparent. Neither said anything. After a week of occasional appearances, Farkas's temper got the better of him.

"What the hell are you doing here?" he demanded. "Do you think I want to see you?" His eyes narrowed and grew dark. "If so, you are dead wrong."

His father looked neither apologetic nor offended. Nor did he look like he was going.

"You never showed the slightest interest in us," continued Farkas. "F*** off, and don't come back."

Upon his father's departure, Farkas felt a sense of victory and also a strange disappointment.

*Couldn't he, at least, explain himself?* he thought. *Better still, say sorry. For God's sake, say sorry.*

One evening, as Farkas walked by the river, he saw his father's reflection in the water.

*I told him to go,* he thought.

He swung around, insults ready. Nobody was there, but the reflection still was. He looked more closely and was shocked to see that it was his own reflection. It is disturbing enough to hold a lifelong grudge against another person. It is much worse to realise that the person is oneself. The grip of anger was loosening, and sorrow was taking its place. Farkas had cried many times for himself but rarely about himself. That would have been too confronting.

A woman appeared and spoke reassuringly to him as if none of this mattered.

"I am Milyaket, Keeper of the Forest," she said. "Your time with us is done. Come with me, please."

Disliking the forest intensely, Farkas followed her. He had nothing to say that was worth saying, so he let Milyaket's soothing voice continue its rhythmic speech.

"We know that you are in pain," said Milyaket. "We will help you get rid of it as soon as it is allowable. You cannot see it now, but your pain saves you from making worse mistakes. You blame others to avoid attacking yourself, but neither is necessary. You are not as you think, and nor is anyone else."

Farkas could not help but soften to Milyaket. She was so calm, peaceful, and good. He saw none of himself in her. That helped. He wanted to keep his forest discovery a secret. Besides, he did not even understand what it all meant.

Milyaket spoke as if she were a consented part of Farkas's thought conversation.

"Anything held in secret cannot be healed," she said. "The light cannot reach that which is locked away in the dark."

They reached a large, open room. Farkas could see very little, but Milyaket acted as if there were things and people everywhere.

"The Advisors have convened," said Milyaket, "and suggest that you return to Earth in human form to continue your journey. They feel that you will make better progress with a body."

"I love a creature that is a spirit," said Farkas. "If I return as a human, we will be too different to connect."

It was the only time he spoke.

"You see the separation of life as very arbitrary at this time," said Milyaket. "You are not alone in this assumption.

You have far more connection than you are even vaguely aware of. You will not lose the love that is yours. Return now."

*In Waldmeer:*

The garden was asleep. It was early winter. Farkas's stride was sure and grounded. Dark hair, well-proportioned body, self-contained face, and eyes that were simultaneously soft and hard.

"It doesn't feel bad to be human," said Farkas. "Let's try this again."

## CHAPTER 4
## WINTER'S OVER

I n Waldmeer:
Winter was coming to a close. Farkas was getting used to being back in a body. He had spent the last few months doing simple tasks and thinking. He looked forward to spring because the warmth would bring the garden back to life. That meant that his little flower friend, Amira, would wake up. He had so much to tell her. She would be surprised that he now had a body. He hoped that she liked his new body. He glanced in the pond to assess it from a flower's point of view. He couldn't tell. Who would know what a flower thinks?

Much of the garden had already awoken and was spreading in all directions. Farkas kept looking at the spot where his favourite friend lived to see if there were any signs of life.

*Strange,* he thought. *I can't remember Amira being a late grower.* A terrible thought crossed his mind. *She isn't asleep. She's dead. She's not coming back.*

Farkas reassured himself with the memory that she had restarted her life as a tiny seed once before.

*She will do that again*, he thought.

She didn't. This time, she didn't come back.

THE SUMMER DAYS were long and warm. There was always a late afternoon sea breeze to sweep away the remaining heat. Everyone in the little town slept with their windows open. The waves, the stars, and the morning birds were the bedmates of all who lived in the village.

Farkas had recently invited another bedmate into his home. Her name was Elise. It did not take long for the village girls to realise that there was a new resident in the cottage on the hill. He was reserved, masculine, striking-looking, and seemed entirely single. Elise, the village's prettiest and most confident girl, marked him as hers. The other girls knew not to challenge her. She had a young, sleek body, long blonde hair, and an infectious smile. Her conversation style was bright and flippant.

At first, Farkas was not interested. However, he soon decided it was ridiculous to grieve over a flower spirit, no matter how close they had been.

*For God's sake,* he thought. *She was a flower. Anyway, she is gone and isn't coming back.*

Besides, he had forgotten that along with a male body comes the drive for a womanly one. Elise was very willing to be that womanly body. And so, Farkas lost himself in her.

It was certainly fun. He even managed to forget his problems somewhat. He started to play with the idea that it might be maintainable and bring him happiness. He reached towards her warm, sleeping body and drew it closer. Elise responded obediently, although she was completely asleep.

Farkas could not help feeling two conflicting ways about her. One was simple, gratuitous pleasure. The other was dislike. He didn't like her. It crossed his mind that he had never felt conflicted about Amira. She loved him purely, and he responded with instinctive devotion. Amira was the only place he felt no conflict. He liked being with her. As for Elise? He liked her body. He liked her smell. He liked her submissive adoration. Nothing about her scared him. Nothing challenged him. He also found her boring, needy, and shallow. She did not love him. She needed him. Her loyalty was to her survival. Farkas knew he was no better. He struggled to find enough love to give to himself, let alone someone else. Yet, he thought there must be something inside him because he could love Amira. That love came from somewhere.

His memory of Amira and his previous life was fading fast. Once he was given a human body, it was surprising that he could remember his spirit existence at all. For some reason, he had retained his memories. They lingered for a while and would soon move into the ether.

After that day with Elise, Farkas could not bring himself to invite her into the house again. Even if he could not have love, he did not have to choose some meaningless, second-rate version of it. It was better to be alone. A few months later, he happened to pass Elise on the street. She didn't see him. She was too busy laughing with her new companion, looking into his eyes as if he were God.

*Yes*, thought Farkas, *it's better to be alone.*

# MARIA OF WALDMEER

# CHAPTER 5
# A GIFT FROM GOD

*In Waldmeer:*

Lenny was a fisherman from Waldmeer. Several generations of his family had lived in the little coastal village. One of his past relatives was a logger, like many men at that time. He had emigrated from Germany. The logging settlement was the spectacular meeting point of forest and stunning coastline. It was he who first referred to the early town as Waldmeer. It means forest-sea in German. The name stuck, and the locals called it that ever since.

At seventeen, Lenny built the small fibro cottage he and his wife had always lived in. It was simple but well cared for and had a lovely, unpretentious garden. It also had an orchard with enough fruit trees for making jam. The bottom of the orchard was home to several hens. There was a large vegetable patch that had fed the family for a few decades. The house was several streets from Farkas, although the two neighbours had not crossed paths. All in all, Lenny and his wife had a relatively smooth life, avoiding many of the difficulties of their neighbours (probably because of their unambitious and genuine approach to everyday life). However, all of that changed a few days ago.

They were now sitting in the country hospital, anxious and weary. With nerves on edge, they were waiting to see what would happen to Maria, their sixteen-year-old daughter. She had been in intensive care for three days. The unthinkable had happened, and she was hit by the school bus on its daily trek along the long, winding coastal road. Her parents' only consolation was that Maria had become immediately unconscious, so they felt she was not in pain.

Many years ago, they had been told that they would not be able to have children. Maria was a wonderful surprise after fifteen years of marriage. They said she was a gift from God (when they would allow themselves such sentimentalities). As if to confirm the hypothesis, Maria was an unusually sweet child with not a mean bone in her body. Her goals in life were simple. She was happy to go to school and help her mother in the small cafe she managed in Waldmeer. Maria was always pleasant to the customers, perhaps a bit dreamy at times, but delightful. She was a genuine asset to the business. She used her earnings to buy little presents for her friends and saved for her future life. Now, it looked like she would not have a future life.

"I am so sorry," said the doctor-in-charge, summoning all his professional training as he entered the hospital room. "I do not think Maria will live past this evening. It is probably best to say your goodbyes."

*IN THE INTER-DIMENSIONAL HOMELAND:*
Maria had almost completely transitioned to the Home-

land. As her parents had hoped, she felt no pain at all. She was quite at peace. Her only concern was the thought that her parents might not be as excited about her leaving as she was.

"Don't worry about your parents," said Maria's inter-dimensional guardian, reassuringly. "It has all been taken care of."

For some reason, as yet unclear, Amira had been given access to this whole Earth drama unfolding. She even saw the accident and watched Maria's guardians look after her as she moved out of her body. They talked to Maria calmly, and there was little stress in the situation for her, despite the great deal of stress in the human world around these same events. Milyaket, Keeper of the Forest, approached Amira.

"We have been so enjoying having you back in the Homeland," said Milyaket, "but, like all of us, you know that in helping others, you find greater happiness yourself."

Amira nodded. She had learned that lesson a long time ago. In the Homeland, where there were many advanced beings, she was frequently reminded how much she still had to learn.

"The Advisors would like to ask you if you are willing to return to Earth in the body of young Maria," Milyaket continued. "She is a suitable match for you, and you will not find her past life or tendencies too grating."

"Of course," said Amira, knowing that whatever the Advisors suggested was always in one's best interest.

"There is one more thing you must know," Milyaket added. "Once you have entered Maria's body, you will not be able to recall your life as you know it now. You will remember Maria's life as if it were your own. Her memory and demeanour will gradually transform into your own

Amira-consciousness. This way, you and Maria's parents will adjust to the change. The timing of this is undecided at this point."

*IN WALDMEER:*

Lenny and his wife could not believe their blessed good fortune when, in the early evening, Maria started to move her arms and open her eyes. She was returning to them.

"Tomorrow," said Lenny for the first and only time ever. "I would like to go to the chapel."

# CHAPTER 6
# WALDMEER CORNER STORE
# AND CAFE

Maria's progress was rapid and unhampered. Everyone in Waldmeer and the surrounding towns knew of the accident and the girl's unexpected recovery. She was soon well enough to do short shifts in the cafe her mother managed, Waldmeer Corner Store and Cafe. It was agreed that it would be best for her to do her remaining year of schooling from home. The townsfolk did not speak of the accident to Maria in case it drew attention to something that might pull her backwards. Instead, they spoke in hushed tones to Maria's mother. They need not have worried. It was only going in one direction.

Farkas was one of the morning coffee visitors to the cafe. He always got takeaway as he couldn't be bothered with other people's annoying civilities. He could barely remember Maria before the accident, but even he was curious about the girl's miraculous recovery. He looked at her closely to see if she really was okay. He was a little embarrassed to find that something about the girl was interesting.

ver the coming year, Farkas gradually started having coffee at the cafe tables. He would read the paper and sometimes talk briefly with Maria's mother, who was not much older than he was. Maria would smile at him when she cleared his table, although she was a bit nervous about the man who lived on the hill. No one in the village seemed to know anything about him, where he came from, how long he was there for, or even what work he did. Farkas certainly wasn't telling anyone anything.

Occasionally, one of the hill-dwellers would ask Maria if she could remember anything from when she was unconscious. Curious to know the answer but too conservative to ask, others would stop talking and listen for the reply. Maria didn't want to disappoint anyone, but could remember nothing.

*Happy birthday, Maria,* Farkas heard one of the cafe regulars say one morning.

"Is it your birthday?" he asked when she brought his coffee. "How old are you?"

The question sounded more important than he intended.

"Eighteen," said Maria.

And something about that answer made Farkas happier than he felt it should have.

MARIA WAS CHANGING. Her parents noticed it and felt it must be a result of the accident. They didn't question her about it as they were grateful to have her with them in any form. Farkas noticed it, too. She was beginning to look older. Perhaps it was the normal change from girl to woman, but it seemed more than that. Her eyes looked like they were searching for something. Previously, Maria never had that look on her face. It did not seem to be the typical restlessness of young adulthood, which pushes the person from the safety of home out into the world's adventure. If it were that, Maria would have been outgrowing the cafe and dreaming of the city. She was content with her work in Waldmeer Corner Store and Cafe. It was a different kind of restlessness. It was the restlessness that comes from inside when one can't quite remember what one is supposed to do.

Farkas also noticed that he was not the only person with a growing interest in Maria. Charlie lived in the back hills of Waldmeer. More than ten years older than Maria and ten years younger than Farkas, her real name was Charmaine, but no one called her that. She had very short, almost shaved, black hair and large, dark eyes that were as intense as Farkas's. She didn't carry the angry or passive-aggressive demeanour that many gay women seem to have. She wasn't masculine, nor was she feminine. She was androgynous and totally owned it. This woman knew what she was doing. She was an up-and-coming artist who already had works in some of the city's galleries. She was unpretentious and treated everyone the same, except for people who annoyed her. She seemed to sense something unusual in Maria, and Farkas could see that Charlie was nurturing it and her. This troubled him as he could not tell what Charlie wanted with Maria.

He knew how to deal with men. You make them feel nervous about challenging you, and they will respect your territory. Women? You flirt with them just enough for them to think you have an interest in them, and then you leave them wanting more. What do you do with someone who thinks differently, comes at things from a different angle, and won't engage in the conflict? Maria liked Charlie. She felt Charlie might have answers to questions she couldn't even form properly.

To add to Farkas's perceived problem, Charlie often came into the cafe with one of her long-term friends, Gabriel. Gabriel was also an artist. He lived in the city and used Charlie's Waldmeer house for sculpting at various times of the year. Charlie and Gabriel were well known and respected in Waldmeer, which was no small achievement given the traditional nature of small country towns. It was common knowledge that Gabriel had had both male and female partners. Unlike Charlie, he was not androgynous. He was very much a man. Both Charlie and Gabriel had an emotional freedom and life courage, which Maria was drawn to. In turn, they sensed the spirit in Maria. After all, they were artists. And artists see the invisible before anyone else.

## CHAPTER 7
## ERDO KAPUS

Maria spent a lot of time in the back hills of Waldmeer. She visited Charlie at her art studio and Gabriel when he was there. Charlie knew a lot about life and people and was generous in sharing it.

"You are too young to know this," Charlie said one afternoon, "but relationships are full of problems. We are drawn to them as if they are the great treasure of life, yet we struggle once we are in them. Those who say otherwise are lying."

She paused and said more kindly, "Not that it's a bad lie, but it's a lie."

As if to redirect her train of thought, Charlie added, "Erdo says that we must try to tell ourselves whenever we feel distressed about our relationships, 'There is another way of looking at this.' What do you think?"

"Who is Erdo?" asked Maria.

"Erdo Kapus. He is my teacher," said Charlie. "He lives in the Leleks."

"What sort of a teacher?"

"The only teacher that matters."

"Who does he teach?"

"Anyone who looks for him."

"In the forest?"

"Yes, the Leleks."

"Does he have a family?"

"No, he is old and lives alone. He says he has a sister, Milyaket, but I have never seen her."

*Milyaket?* thought Maria.

A memory stirred, but it was so far away that she had no hope of gathering it.

"Has Gabriel ever been to see Erdo?" asked Maria.

"No," said Charlie, "but I often tell him what Erdo tells me. Gabriel and I have a joke when we think someone is being egotistical. 'That's ego, not Erdo.' It's a lame joke, but we both find it funny for some reason. I don't think Gabriel believes everything I tell him, but he always listens."

"Can you take me to see Erdo?" asked Maria. "Will he see me?"

"I will take you," said Charlie, "but it's not for me to say who he will see."

"Will you tell him I would like to come," asked Maria.

"There is no need to tell him," said Charlie. "He will know. He will either be there or not."

*IN THE LELEKS:*

The following week, Charlie drove Maria an hour into the Leleks, the large forested area behind Waldmeer. Erdo lived in a part of the forest that was not a national park, but no one else seemed to own it. It was slow driving because the dirt track was bumpy and windy, even though it wasn't that far. Charlie parked the car at the narrow walking bridge.

"Aren't you coming?" asked Maria.

"No, he only likes one person to visit at a time," said Charlie. "He says it's less distracting for us. Walk over the hill. If he is coming, he will be there."

He wasn't there. Maria sat on a log by the pond and listened to the birds.

"What would you like to ask?" said a voice behind her.

She turned to see who had spoken. Erdo was supposedly old, but he looked like he could be any age over forty. Suddenly, Maria could not think of one single question worth asking. Erdo was so still that there didn't seem to be anything important enough to ask that would be worth breaking the silence for. It was Erdo himself who spoke in the manner of continuing a conversation that had started a long time ago.

"Everything that comes from this world is problematic," he said. "That is because this world is the upside-down of the real world. It is a suffering one. I will give you a choice today. If you prefer, you can leave and go gently into the real world, and there you will be spared much suffering, and you will only feel happiness. Think carefully. Your choice will determine your path."

Erdo left her at the pond and said he would return soon. The pond was idyllic. Everything was glowing with light and beauty, and so profoundly peaceful that it was inconceivable that anything could take away from the gorgeous bliss.

*Who would not want to be so beautifully happy and fulfilled?* thought Maria.

She became increasingly unaware of her body and felt

merged with all the living things around her. She was fast losing awareness of who she was in that other tiny, dysfunctional world of strange bodies fighting with themselves and each other.

After some time, Maria saw two spectacular black swans land balletically on the pond and swim harmoniously amongst the water lilies. They were not asking anything from each other, yet they were together.

*People are so separate in that other little world,* thought Maria.

"The darkness uses relationships to keep people revolving around the ego's demands," said Erdo, who had returned.

"If relationships cause people so much angst and heartbreak," said Maria, "wouldn't it be better to forget about them and only think of the real world?"

"In the beginning, people see the beauty of the divine in each other," explained Erdo. "They are captivated and delighted by it, but quickly forget what they once saw as fear reclaims its supremacy. So begins the fight to protect oneself and one's rightful claims. What is owed becomes paramount. Guilt becomes the preferred tool of manipulation. Freedom is lost in the battle. Love is forgotten. What is left are the rare moments of peace and forgiveness, which somehow save the day."

Erdo cheerfully turned to Maria and said, "And what will it be? Are you staying or going?"

Maria couldn't help feeling that Erdo knew the answer, but he was waiting for a reply.

"Seeing as I am already here, I will stay," said Maria. "Maybe someone needs me."

"Many need you." Erdo smiled warmly. "And you need them. We do not get to Heaven alone. Charlie is waiting for you on the other side of the bridge. You have kept her waiting long enough."

"We don't want her getting angry," he added as if Charlie were a naughty puppy.

∽

*In Waldmeer:*

A few days later, in the cafe, Maria overheard two locals talking about the old man and his recent sightings in the Leleks.

"Yeah, right, in ya' dreams, mate," both laughed with the good-natured superiority that keeps mates together 'cause they know better.

"Have you ever seen the old man who lives in the forest, Farkas?" Maria ventured.

"Yeah, I have," said Farkas.

Maria was surprised.

"I've seen him a few times when I've been near the old bridge," said Farkas.

"Have you spoken to him?"

"He gestured to me, both times I've seen him, to cross the bridge."

"And did you?" asked Maria.

"Of course not. I don't trust him," Farkas snapped angrily.

He pushed his chair out, almost knocking Maria over, and left abruptly. He looked as angry with Maria as he was about the old man.

Maria wanted to cry, but couldn't because she was at work.

*Farkas does a lot of blaming and shaming,* she thought. *Those in pain give pain.*

As for Farkas, he stopped coming to the cafe.

# THE LELEKS

## CHAPTER 8
## FAMILY

Ever since Farkas stormed out of the cafe, not to return, Maria felt ill. She was even finding some of the cafe customers annoying. Mrs Reisenden was one of them. Maria's mother liked her and enjoyed talking with her whenever she visited Waldmeer.

"You have returned," said Maria's mother with obvious delight. "Do tell me how life has been in the city since you last were here on holiday."

Mrs Reisenden would often bring Maria's mother a little present, and she would tell her all about the cultural events she had been attending.

"Maria, dear, please bring Verloren's coffee over," said Maria's mother. "I will sit here and chat with her as we haven't had the pleasure of her company for a while."

She turned to Verloren and said, "This morning, I walked past the old cottage on the hill. I recalled that several summers ago, you did some gardening work there. They were so lucky to have you!"

"You are too kind," said Verloren.

Verloren had mixed memories of her time at the house but could not recall exactly why.

"Does it have a new person living there now?" Said Verloren. "I must introduce myself to them."

*Mrs Reisenden must have been the gardener at Farkas's house before he moved in,* thought Maria.

"I enjoyed my time at that house," said Verloren. "It was good to do some manual gardening again. We have to keep grounded, you know. We can't be high and mighty."

Maria gave Mrs Reisenden her coffee. As she turned to walk away, she rolled her eyes, which was quite unlike her. Maria loved her mother, but the difference in their tastes was becoming markedly wider. Perhaps that was only obvious to Maria and not to her mother.

As Maria was still not feeling well, she decided to visit Erdo.

"Your body would not get sick if you held no thought of resentment," said Erdo, as if this were elementary knowledge. "It is neither good nor bad in itself. If you use it to bless, it will not complain. If we hold anything against anyone, we will suffer ourselves."

*That is not easy, but perhaps I could take it on board,* thought Maria. *At least I wouldn't feel sick anymore, so it's probably worth it.*

"More than this," continued Erdo, "you are the very people you dislike."

"I am not those people," said Maria.

This was getting offensive.

"I am not those people," she repeated with a fire rising inside her.

Erdo, who usually knew everything, was unexplainably mistaken in this instance.

"I am not Farkas with his stupid, angry attitude pushing everyone away as if they all want to kill him," said Maria. "I am not that bare-boobed girl, Elise, running around town sleeping with anyone she thinks she can get something from. She must think she has nothing to offer but a body to be used and discarded. I am not that woman from the city, Verloren Reisenden. She acts like she is so kind, but she lies to her husband, chases good-looking men, and spends her time shopping and talking to her friends about how badly life is treating her."

Maria's anger was replaced with a calmer, older Maria who spoke with authority. "Those women, her friends, come together under the guise of love to gossip about innocent people who have what they do not: happiness. And if they cannot drag the person into their weak world of suffering, they will seek retribution. How little they realise that their great bond of love will so easily be turned against each other."

Erdo remained silent for some time and then spoke to the younger Maria, "You are all those people. If one is left behind, none of us gets there. No one can be forgotten. We are connected as one creation with many interrelated parts. We are family. Whoever you hold accountable for their mistaken identity holds you in the dream."

*That's too hard,* thought Maria.

"If it were too hard, you would not be hearing this now," said Erdo. "We hear what we are ready to hear. We draw into our lives those who will help us to grow. Naturally, we tend to have mixed feelings about those very people, but they are marked for us, and we invited them into our house. We have forgotten that we wrote them an invitation some time ago. We look at them as if they are intruders when, all along, they are guests."

MARIA BUMPED into Farkas a few days later while walking to the shops.

"Hello, Maria," said Farkas, who acted like there was no reason not to be friendly, although to Maria, there seemed to be many.

*Maybe he wants something,* thought Maria.

"I hear you are spending a lot of time in the hills with Charlie?" said Farkas.

"Yes," said Maria. "I am with Gabriel as much as Charlie. Charlie and I talk about Erdo, the old man in the forest. Gabriel and I talk about life."

Maria was being far more generous with information about her private life than she felt she should be.

"Gabriel? The gay guy from the city?" asked Farkas.

"Yes," said Maria. "Do you know him?"

Farkas nodded that he knew him, but looked like he did not want to know him any more than he already did. There didn't seem to be anything else that Maria could say to re-divert a conversation headed nowhere good. Farkas had decided that the conversation was over. He turned to leave.

"By the way," he added, "a lady, Verloren, called in at my house. She said she used to do gardening there before I moved in. She also said she would call again."

*Call again?* Maria thought. *It is surprising Farkas let her call once.*

"She comes to the cafe," said Maria. "My mother likes her. Erdo says I must like her too."

She said this as if she were a child being corrected by a parent.

"Are you sure that's what he meant?" Farkas asked with surprising wisdom. "The woman, Verloren, said gardening was good for her because it made her forget about herself and her problems."

*That was honest of Mrs Reisenden,* Maria thought. *It's rather strange of Farkas to have such a conversation with her. He hardly talks to anyone, let alone someone like her.*

For a moment, Maria and Farkas looked at each other as if both were trying to recollect things they could not recall: invisible bonds and an unclear purpose. As neither could remember, they returned to their usual demeanour and said goodbye.

## CHAPTER 9
## HOLD MY HAND

G abriel was a relatively free thinker. He wasn't one of those gay guys who acts like a girl (and a stupid girl at that).

*Don't we have enough stupid girls,* Maria sometimes thought, *without the gay guys adding to the population?*

He was also not on remote control of marriage, mortgage, and kids, hoping that the masses might know what they were doing. He might not have answers, but he had questions. Perhaps that was why he was an artist. He looked for answers in his art. He mostly worked as a sculptor, so he was used to using his hands. They were interesting hands—purposeful like a carpenter but soft like a musician. Sometimes, he took hold of Maria's hand when they walked along Merri Creek, which ran through Charlie's hillside property. As he was generally affectionate, it seemed natural enough, and neither said anything about it. They just enjoyed it: walking together, listening to the wind, watching the water, and calmly talking about life. It made Maria think about the body and how we connect through touch.

~

"OH, DON'T ASK ME THAT," said Charlie when Maria asked her what she thought was the best approach to sexual relationships. "I have had problems in all my relationships."

Maria sensed that Charlie was about to go on an extended elaboration of all those problems.

"What does Erdo say?" she quickly asked.

Charlie turned her thoughts to Erdo. "He says that we use sex as a way of trying to complete ourselves because we are so fragmented."

*That doesn't sound very encouraging,* thought Maria.

"He also says that we are drawn to people who have something we need," said Charlie. "We think we will be able to gain the coveted thing by uniting with them."

*Oh, that sounds even worse,* thought Maria.

"Does he say anything good about it?" she asked.

"Yes, he does," said Charlie. "He says that even though our most prized personal bondings are generally selfish and egocentric, they are also our saviour. Through them, we learn to see the essence of ourselves, the other, and life. Our relationships are transformed, and so are we. 'Offer your relationships to God, and you will not be disappointed with what is made of them,' he says."

Maria pondered that most people wanted to use sex for their own purposes, not be used by it for a purpose other than the one they had in mind.

*Life is tricky,* she thought. *Maybe it is not so much deceptive as it is wise and kind and knows how to get our attention.*

That thought satisfied her, and she felt it was a direction to head towards.

ONE MORNING, Maria was walking with Gabriel as they had arranged to meet for coffee while he was in Waldmeer. They decided not to go to Maria's workplace, Waldmeer Corner Store and Cafe. There was only one other decent cafe in town. As Farkas no longer went to the cafe Maria worked in, he got his coffee from the other cafe and walked out the door as Gabriel and Maria walked in.

"Hello, Farkas. You know Gabriel, of course," said Maria cheerfully.

The air was thickening quickly. After a tense hello on both sides, Farkas decided he was not quite finished with the conversation.

"How are things in the city with the boys?" Farkas asked with obvious ill intent.

Gabriel raised his eyebrows slightly and spoke in a slow and deliberate voice.

"Yeah, good, thanks. How about you, Farkas?" said Gabriel, pronouncing Farkas as F U C K A R S E instead of Farkas.

*Oh my God*, thought Maria. *That's a red flag to a bull. This is getting serious.*

She looked at both men, neither of whom was paying the slightest bit of attention to her. They were way too interested in insulting each other. Suddenly, it all seemed terribly funny. She couldn't help but laugh. Both men were surprised and annoyed that she was interrupting them. They looked at her as if to say, *Why are you even standing there? And, anyway, you're really too weird sometimes.* Nevertheless, the tension had been broken.

"I don't know why I was given such a ridiculous name,"

Farkas suddenly said with a smile. "I have enough trouble in life without having to fight every Tom, Dick, and Harry for my dignity."

Maria took the opportunity to leave her two friends.

"I'll catch you later, Gabriel," said Maria.

Halfway down the street, she glanced towards them and saw that they were tentatively chatting.

*Perhaps not best friends,* she thought, *but with the respect that is due.*

# CHAPTER 10
# NIGHTMARE

It had been raining all week in Waldmeer. Some of the roads had closed due to landslides, and there was mud everywhere. Maria had been having nightmares. On the way to see Erdo, she had a foreboding feeling, which was made worse by his not being there when she arrived. She crossed the rampaging river and walked up the hill from where Erdo typically came. The forest was getting darker.

*It must be going to rain again,* she thought.

The nightmare was creeping in. Sensing it, she walked more slowly until her footsteps were silent and carefully made their way through the trees, lest she offend the approaching enemy. She didn't want to continue, but going back seemed as daunting as going forward.

As soon as she reached the top of the hill, she stopped dead in her tracks. A dense and terrible power was coming up from the valley and moving towards her. The nightmare was back and far worse than before. This was out of her depth. It seemed all the evil in this world and more. She felt it intended to sweep her up effortlessly with barely a glance, crush every bone in her body, and drop her to die painfully somewhere below. Terror immobilised both her body and mind.

*Wake up*, she heard herself say.

This time, there was no waking up because she wasn't asleep. She was a tiny leaf about to be brutally crushed. As the pressure from the monster was closing in on her, a distant memory called from deep within her.

*Maria, it is I,* said a female voice. *I am with you. I know this monster. It is defeatable. Listen carefully to me. You made the monster. Now, unmake it.*

The voice was familiar, yet Maria didn't know who it was. At this point, it didn't matter.

"Unmake it? How? I am terrified, and it is crushing me," said Maria.

*Stand your ground. Do not close your eyes. Look at it,* said the voice.

Maria looked. It was horrible: suffering and pain.

*Look deeper,* said the voice. *It is the world that you and your brothers and sisters have created. It is but a nightmare.*

As Maria looked more closely, her terror started to soften.

*Let it be blown away as nothing,* said the voice. *I am here waiting for you.*

"Let it be blown away as nothing. I am here waiting for you," repeated Maria.

The darkness was breaking up. Maria's body was no longer under pressure. The trees were becoming visible. The sun started to glisten on the wet leaves. There settled a sense of harmony, peace, and safety. Maria felt it would be impossible for anything ever to hurt her again.

Erdo walked over the hill as if nothing had happened. "I'm sorry I'm late. Did you need me?"

"I'm fine, thanks," said Maria. "I'll be going home now."

As she calmly and gratefully walked back to her car, she sensed that she was becoming a different person and had aged many years, perhaps many lifetimes, in those few moments. She had never felt so well, hopeful, and content.

"Well done, Amira," Erdo called out to Maria as he waved from the top of the hill.

*Amira?* thought Maria. *Erdo is old. Sometimes, he gets his students' names muddled up.*

# THE CALL TO LOVE

## CHAPTER 11
## NOBLE

Maria was turning twenty-one, and it had been more than four years since her accident. Her mother, Lucy, noticed she seemed to have aged many years, particularly in the last few months.

"Truth be told, at twenty-one," Lucy said to her husband, "she knows more than you and I will ever know."

Most of Lucy's friends loved Maria. They still saw her as the sweet little girl given to Lucy and Lenny later in their marriage, who recovered from a terrible accident. They never bothered to look and see if Maria had grown up. Perhaps it was better that way.

Being a more recent friend, Verloren was different. She could see who Maria was. Maria was what Verloren was not. Verloren was nice to Maria whenever Lucy was present, but as soon as Lucy was out of sight, she would dismiss Maria as if she were not worth acknowledging.

These days, Lucy often found herself asking her daughter for advice.

One afternoon in the cafe, Lucy said to Maria, "Verloren was teary today when she told me about her marriage. She gets interested in other men, which never works out, and then she gets even more upset. I don't know what to say. Do you think you could help her?"

"I would love to help her," said Maria, "but she wouldn't listen to me. She might listen to you, though."

"What will I tell her?" asked Lucy.

"Tell her that her husband loves her as best as he can," said Maria, "but everyone is absorbed in their own worries. And tell her not to look for other men because they won't be able to make her happy either."

"I can't tell her that," said Lucy. "She'll never speak to me again."

"Well, it's the truth," laughed Maria. "She thinks she can make herself feel better by gaining the love of someone she admires."

"Don't we all think that?" asked Lucy without shame.

"Yes, Mamma, we do," said Maria. "And it doesn't work for anyone."

ANOTHER EVENING, Lucy and Maria were standing in their kitchen peeling vegetables for dinner.

"Why is Farkas so angry with us?" Lucy asked. "I don't mind that he doesn't come to our cafe anymore. I'm not offended, but whenever I see him on the street, he acts as if I asked him to leave, and he won't even say hello. It makes me sad because I don't hold anything against anyone. Anyway, he came to our cafe for a long time and..."

Lucy paused, searching for the right words, "...and I miss him."

"Don't worry," said Maria. "It's just him. In his mind, everyone has or is going to hurt him. He is protecting himself."

"Why would he think that?" asked Lucy. "He must have friends who love him. Everyone has friends."

"Do they?" said Maria. "Most have arrangements."

The conversation was getting too much for Lucy.

"Okay, darling," she said, "please get the hens' eggs and bring some lettuce back with you from the garden."

After dinner, Maria walked the few streets to Farkas's house and left some eggs at his front door with a note saying,

*These are from Mum. She said that she misses seeing you at the cafe.*

Maria thought, *If Mum knew I said that, she would kill me.* She laughed and ran home.

A few days later, Farkas came to get his morning coffee from Waldmeer Corner Store and Cafe. He ordered take-away, chatted with Lucy about how good she looked, and then went outside to wait for the order.

"I'll take it to him," Maria said when his name was called.

"Thank you," said Farkas when Maria handed him his coffee.

He then added, surprisingly, "I hate my name. I would like myself better if I had a better name."

"It's a beautiful name," said Maria. "It means *wolf*. I know this because wolves are my favourite creatures. They don't like fighting but are fierce if they need to be. They are very connected to their pack and will be loyal until death. They have all the intelligence and sensitivity of a dog but much more. They are noble creatures. Why would you want to change that?"

# CHAPTER 12
# NO ONE CAN TAKE HER

*In the Leleks:*

I Maria looked straight into Erdo's eyes and said, "I know who Amira is. I know why you called me that name last time I was here. She helped me with the nightmare. She talks to me all the time nowadays."

"Yes," said Erdo. "Is that a problem?"

"Yes, it is," said Maria. "I hear Amira's voice so often, I think she is taking me over."

"And is *that* a problem?" asked Erdo.

"Yes," said Maria. "I want to get rid of her."

"I see," said Erdo without emotion.

"Amira is not from this world," said Maria. "She doesn't belong here. She will destroy my life. She doesn't give this life any value. I don't think she even wants to stay here. I won't be able to be a normal person. And I won't even be here much longer. She will take us both away."

"I see," said Erdo.

"I'm scared," said Maria.

"I can see that."

"I'm sorry. I know it's not what you want, but it's too much for me."

Erdo was not often sympathetic but said, "It's alright. No one is asking anything of you that you would not want for yourself. You are free. No one has to be a martyr. The powers that be are not interested in sacrifices."

Maria relaxed. "Oh, okay. Well, that is alright then."

"I have an idea," Erdo said enthusiastically. "Why don't you leave Amira here with me. She and I can have a good ol' catch-up, and she will wait for you in case you want her back."

"That sounds like a wonderful idea," said Maria. "I will leave her here with you."

She frowned slightly. "She will be safe, won't she? I wouldn't want anything to happen to her. No one will take her away?"

Erdo laughed.

"Trust me. No one can take her from me." He walked off as if he thought that was the most amusing thing he had heard in ages.

With delighted relief, Maria drove back to Waldmeer feeling like a normal person, a twenty-one-year-old girl, instead of a ten-thousand-and-twenty-one-year-old sage.

# CHAPTER 13
# ON MY OWN

It was true that Maria no longer had to deal with the challenges Amira brought into her life. However, she did not foresee that much of the life she loved had been created by Amira, not by her. Those parts of her life were fast dismantling.

Without Amira, Maria was a kind, uncomplicated, and natural young woman, but nothing more. For all Farkas's resisting it, the thing that drew him to Maria was Amira. Amira could help him in a way that he could not help himself. She saw him as he truly was. On the other hand, Maria could only see what was before her eyes. Farkas had no need for a twenty-one-year-old girl in his life. He could run rings around such a person.

Maria hardly saw Farkas in town anymore. Sometimes, she walked past his house on the hill to see if there was any life there. It looked like no one was ever home, but she couldn't be sure. Maybe he had gone away. Perhaps he was sitting in his house, being a recluse. Maybe he was having a fabulous time doing all sorts of fun things. Wherever he was, he had made himself invisible to her.

As for Gabriel, he soon noticed the change in Maria. He didn't know why it happened, but he knew he felt bored around her. Too kind to tell her the truth, he casually mentioned, one day, that he had lots of work in the city. Charlie told Maria that Gabriel was busy with his city friends. Whatever he was busy with, it wasn't Waldmeer or Maria.

*I guess Gabriel doesn't need the friendship of a young country girl who has only ever worked in the local cafe,* Maria thought.

She would see him from the cafe window when he was in town on the odd occasion.

*He didn't let me know he was here,* she thought sadly.

Maria supposed it was a consolation that Elise and the other girls of Waldmeer also had lost interest in her. They no longer bothered to give her sideways glances, speak in hushed tones, or look straight past her as she passed them on the street. It seemed no longer necessary to undermine her.

Although a little puzzled by Maria's sudden character reversal, Lucy and Lenny had become used to the unexpected from Maria. They decided it was best to go with the flow. It was their saving grace in life.

Charlie still loved Maria, but these days, she talked to her more as a little sister than as an equal. Or perhaps, rather than as an equal, it would be more correct to say that Charlie previously treated Maria like a rarity (such as one finds in an old op shop to be treasured).

It was a revelation to Maria that even though people could find the Amira part of her uncomfortable, unpredictable, annoying or illogical, it was also the part in which people had the most faith. Their faith was not misplaced. Amira loved the most, forgave the most, understood the most, laughed the most, and had the most to give. Those who felt they had too much to lose from Amira's presence targeted her as an enemy. Now, both friends and enemies were gone.

Maria didn't blame anyone for losing interest in her; she even found herself somewhat lifeless and lost. She wasn't exactly unhappy with herself, but she felt she was a shadow of the person she had been.

She started walking on the beach after work, looking for something. The waves rolled in, one after the other, peaceful in their constancy. Maria needed silence. She got it.

# CHAPTER 14
# THE LONG BEACH

As Maria walked on the long beaches of Waldmeer, she often felt alone. She felt alone both on and off the beach. It was not entirely true that she was alone because she still had Erdo, Charlie, her mother, and father. Yet, she *was* alone. No Amira. No Farkas. No Gabriel. She wondered why it would matter so much that Farkas and Gabriel were both gone. For quite a while, she hardly saw Farkas. When she did, his anger hovered just below the surface, ready to emerge if she did or said anything he felt warranted it. And Gabriel? Why did it matter that he didn't have time for Maria anymore? She always knew he had a full and busy life in the city.

*Why are they so important to me to be such a loss?* thought Maria. *I didn't choose them to be in my life.*

They certainly would not have been obvious choices. One could be feral, and the other lived in a different world.

*If I didn't choose them, maybe they chose me?* she thought.

They would have as little chosen her as she would have chosen them.

*Who made the choice, then?* Maria wondered. *These choices seem to be made on their own. They bring as much sorrow as joy. Maybe more. Why? Are they designed to hurt us? Perhaps they bring hidden grace, but we struggle to find it.*

Maria looked at the seagulls powering low over the wild beach. Her mind was very still and quiet.

*It is the light of love that connects us to others,* she thought. *That is what we miss. We miss the love. We answer the call of love. It comes from God and touches our souls.*

These were deep thoughts. Perhaps Amira was close by.

*It is one thing to lose people you love,* thought Maria. *It is another to lose yourself. That is a greater loss.*

"Life is not worth much to me without Amira," Maria called to the seagulls as they sat on the sand. "Even if I have no one else, I must, at least, have her."

The seagulls lifted in one communal effort and turned to sea.

She called after them, "I will get her back."

# RETRIEVING AMIRA

# CHAPTER 15
# NORTH COUNTRY

*In the Leleks:*

"What do you mean she's not here?" said Maria. "You told me that no one would take her."

"Of course, no one took her," said Erdo. "She left of her own accord. She said she wanted to visit the North Country and see her friends in the Garden of Garourinn."

"But I want her back," said Maria.

"Calm down. You will have her back. My sister, Milyaket, is visiting me at the moment. She is the keeper of another forest. On her way home, she will happily take you to the North Country, and you can retrieve Amira."

"My parents will worry if I am gone for long," said Maria.

"I will send a message to them that you will be staying the week with Charlie," said Erdo. "That will be long enough."

*I hope so,* thought Maria.

"Thank you," she said. "It is quiet in the cafe, so my mother will be fine."

"Milyaket has all you need for the journey," said Erdo. "You will start immediately."

*I*N THE INTER-DIMENSIONAL *N*ORTH *C*OUNTRY:

Although Maria had never met Milyaket, she felt instantly familiar and comfortable.

*She is Erdo's sister*, thought Maria.

She had much she wanted to ask Milyaket. In particular, she was curious about Erdo and Milyaket's family.

*What sort of family is that?* she wondered.

However, after a few words of introduction, Milyaket remained utterly silent and would not be drawn into any conversation. After numerous attempts, Maria accepted that the journey would be a silent one.

"When will we get there?" asked Maria.

"We will know," said Milyaket.

*Strange answer,* thought Maria.

Maria and Milyaket walked for several days. Milyaket had arranged for them to stay somewhere simple and safe each evening. Maria wondered who owned the little huts deep in the forest. As Milyaket was silent, Maria had no other place to go but into her thoughts.

As each hour passed, her thoughts became quieter and more organised. And as her thoughts became more tranquil, Maria noticed that the physical terrain changed somewhat. Milyaket's silence had a hypnotising effect. It was a rhythmical silence: steady, assured, joyous, and purposeful. It was a meditation in itself. Sometimes, Maria forgot to think about what they were doing and where they were going. She didn't forget out of distraction or weariness. She was feeling acutely awake and alive.

By the third afternoon, the landscape had changed entirely, and they approached a mountain pass.

"We are here," said Milyaket. "We are entering the North Country. You will not need me from here. Go straight through the pass, and you will find the Garden of Garourinn on the other side. May the Great Ones be with you."

Maria would have been scared alone, except that her mind had become so quiet that fear seemed inappropriate. She tried to keep the same peaceful state of mind as she walked, but without Milyaket, it seemed much harder to do.

## CHAPTER 16
## PACK

It was early evening, and Maria didn't seem to be getting any closer to the end of the pass. She was warm enough as it was summer and relatively mild in the mountain air. She felt it wisest to get off the main path and find a sheltered spot for the night. Sitting in the fading light, she ate some of the food Milyaket had given her.

Suddenly, an uneasy stillness fell all around. The trees, the small animals, the wind, and even the plants all held their breath as if waiting to see the outcome of an impending event. Maria looked around her nervously and then gasped. A pack of about thirty wolves was circling her with eyes glued not to her meagre bits of food but to her.

*I am the food*, she thought.

Running would have been ridiculous. This pack was made of healthy, strong, vibrant creatures—masters of their terrain. Still terrified, an idea entered the tiny bit of still mind that was left in Maria from her journey.

*I love dogs. They are my friends. Wolves are ancient dogs. There is nothing to fear.*

The largest wolf approached Maria and, to her surprise, she could understand him.

"You are Maria? My name is Galahad," said the wolf. "This is my pack. We guard the borders of Garourinn. We will keep you safe for the rest of your journey. We are travelling further north to the far border of Garourinn. Night is soon upon us. Come with us."

Not waiting for an answer, Galahad nodded for his pack to fall into line. The injured and elderly went first. This seemed a little mean to Maria, as they would be the most vulnerable to attack. However, she later found out that they set the pace. Some of the stronger males followed close behind them. Many of the females and young took their place in the centre ahead of the remaining male wolves. Some distance behind walked Galahad on his own.

One of the bitches approached Maria and said, "My name is Sage. I am Galahad's mate. Walk with me."

It was almost dark, so they stopped at a cave for the night. A few of the hunters went out looking for nocturnal creatures. They soon came back with meat. Since her accident, Maria had been vegetarian. She couldn't eat cooked meat, let alone raw meat.

The wolves respected their prey's life and counted it as being as worthy as their own. They would accept their death as they did the death of their food. They did not give more importance to one life than another. Further, there was a sense that the Great Order of Life was to be trusted and that nothing could ever be taken from anyone that was rightfully theirs. Maria ate the last of the food she had.

The next day, Sage and the other bitches showed her where to find berries and various fruits. It looked like she was going to be with them some days. Each night, the pack stayed close, both for warmth and affection. Maria was happily included as if she belonged. The invisible threads of togetherness were ever-present amongst the wolves. They were not possessive, controlling or needy. There was a simple order that everyone accepted for the pack's good. They found their happiness and stability in the well-being of all. Unlike humans, the wolves were instinctively oriented in one direction only—to whatever made a harmonious and well-functioning community.

*Perhaps they are like the angels,* Maria thought. *Angels also don't have a choice. They are divine because that's the only way they can be.*

## CHAPTER 17
## BORDER

Galahad came from the back of the pack and took his stride beside Maria.

*He must have something important to tell me,* she thought.

He and the other wolves treated Maria as one who was not fully aware of their rightful inheritance.

"We will soon be at the entrance to the Garden of Garourinn," said Galahad. "We will leave you there as we cannot enter the garden. It is a privilege only for those who have the Spark of God in them."

"But you do have that spark," said Maria.

"It is our task to serve those with the spark," said Galahad. "In so doing, one day, we may earn it ourselves. One of our ancestors sacrificed his life to save a baby human not far from here. He was badly wounded in a battle with a wolf from a foreign pack, but he managed to keep the child safe. He carried it to the border of Garourinn, where it was gratefully accepted. He did not know that it was the youngest child of the Head Gardener. In return, our ancestor wolf was given the Spark of God. He died from his wounds but was then reborn as a human and began his long journey in a different dimension."

"That's beautiful," said Maria, "but he may have been better off staying as a wolf. You wolves are happy. Most humans are not."

"No," said Galahad. "It is a great honour to be human. Humans can freely choose their destiny and, one day, will all choose the right destiny. We do not have that choice. Farewell, it has been my happy duty to serve you."

"The honour has been all mine," said Maria with restrained emotion.

One doesn't crumble in front of an alpha wolf. They are too dignified. Each wolf came up, in turn, and rubbed its head on Maria's leg. Then, they turned as a pack and fell into place. She felt she would truly miss them and wished she could have a pack of wolves back home in Waldmeer, but that would hardly work.

MARIA HAD BEEN SITTING at the border of Garourinn for several hours. Not only did Amira not come, but neither did anyone else. She rested under a tree and drifted into a contented sleep. She could feel the filtered sun radiating from above. She dreamed that Amira was talking to her.

"Don't you think we have waited here long enough?" said Amira. "We have things to do back home."

It dawned on her that all her walking with Milyaket had called Amira back into her being. Every step she took deeper into silence brought Amira closer to her soul. And her time with the wolves, when she had become so aligned with the pack and the rhythm of nature, stabilised Amira's presence even more. By the time Maria and the pack had reached the border of Garourinn, Amira was completely reestablished within her.

While still asleep, Maria dreamed that she was resting on the back of a large, flying creature. Maybe it was an angel. The wind was rapidly pushing past her, but she wasn't cold. It was beautifully warm and cosy in a nest of softness.

*IN WALDMEER:*

The following day, Maria woke in her bed in Waldmeer.

"Nice to have you back again, darling," said Lucy, kissing her daughter. "We always miss you, even though you are only in the back hills. It has been quiet at the cafe, but we will be busy today. I will be glad of your help."

Maria could remember every detail of her trip to the North Country. Her travels were no longer disappearing into the ether.

## CHAPTER 18
## SEEING

*In Waldmeer:*

Since Maria had retrieved Amira, they lived side by side in a more compatible way. Each would speak at a different time. Maria could now distinguish the two and choose which would get a voice. Previously, she had trouble even recognising who was who. It was a satisfactory arrangement, although both knew that, in the end, one of them would win. Although Amira was many times more powerful, it was part of the arrangement that she would not be allowed to come forward unless invited by Maria. And Maria had to grow into Amira.

When Amira first entered Maria, she acquired all of Maria's memories, tendencies, longings, and pains. She also took on humanity's collective memories, tendencies, longings, and pains, as we all do. Amira had to work with what she had inherited, and Maria had to learn to want Amira freely. There was no hurry. The destination was sure. The timing was up to Maria.

GABRIEL WAS BACK. Maria asked him what he had been doing in the city.

"Not much," was the extent of Gabriel's reply.

He was back, but he was back in a different way. He was more directive. He sometimes got angry with Maria. It wasn't necessarily a bad thing. It meant that he trusted she would still be there.

Sometimes, when he wanted to put her in her place, he would say, "You are young. You have barely been away from Waldmeer. You have never even had a boyfriend. No offence, but there are lots of things you have no idea about."

To make sure that she got the point, he added, "And half the time, you live in a fantasy world. God only knows where."

Maria didn't mind. She had a power inside her. Who needs to quibble about details? She felt that Amira's temporary departure from her life was not the only cause of Gabriel's recent absence.

"Look," Gabriel said one afternoon, "I am a straightforward person. We all have friends. I have many. And you are entitled to be friends with whoever you want, but I don't like Farkas. I don't trust him. If you want to be friends with him, don't expect too much from me."

"I don't see Farkas anymore," said Maria.

Gabriel took no notice of her reply. It didn't seem to matter if she saw him or not. Maria tried to make light of the situation and made a joke. Gabriel didn't laugh.

She put her hand on his shoulder and said, "Everything is fine. Please don't worry about this."

Gabriel removed her hand.

She tried being firm and said, "This is silly."

Gabriel said, "I don't think so."

AN ADVANTAGE of having Amira back was that Maria found it was not as necessary to make the trip to the Leleks to see Erdo as often as she used to. She could tune into Amira. One evening, on the beach, she did just that about her recent conversation with Gabriel.

"This seems to me a no-win situation," said Maria. "I want Gabriel to be happy, but to make him happy, I have to accept his way of seeing life, which has problems. Besides, will it even make him happy? I doubt it."

"True," said Amira. "We all see a different reality and make decisions based on what we see. Everyone is trying to protect their interests in the best way possible. The world is commonly viewed as a place where someone must lose for someone else to win. It's a competition with winners and losers. This is particularly so in one's most valued relationships."

The sea was gentle. The waves were regular and soothing.

"You must know in your own heart," continued Amira, "that there is an overriding Love that loves everyone. Life is not a competition. No one has to lose for someone else to win. A true blessing blesses everyone. A fragmented love that makes others lose will eventually turn upon itself and destroy the very thing that was so carefully guarded. An open-hearted love will follow a course that can only lead somewhere good. Know that for yourself. Know it for Gabriel. And know it for everyone else, without exception."

# HEALING

# CHAPTER 19
# DAUGHTER

"We are seeing you every weekend at the moment," Lucy said to Verloren.

"Yes, I have made an ongoing arrangement with Farkas," said Verloren.

Maria's ears picked up. She didn't have a good feeling in her stomach.

"I am doing a project with his garden," said Verloren, "and I will use it as a feature in one of our magazines. I come to Waldmeer every weekend now as there is a great deal to do, and I have huge plans."

"That's terrific for Farkas," said Lucy. "He gets free gardening. Who wouldn't want that?"

"Yes, it's a little more than that," said Verloren somewhat sheepishly (although sheepish was not in Verloren's nature). "We are paying him considerably because otherwise, he wouldn't do it."

Returning to her confident, bouncy self, she added, "It's all worth it because I want that particular garden, and the result will be stunning."

The feeling in Maria's stomach got worse.

That evening, at dinner, Lucy told her husband about Verloren's project in Farkas's garden.

"Yeah, I already know," said Lenny. "Farkas's neighbour told me. I don't get it. Who would pay to work in someone else's garden? Does she fancy him or somethin'?"

"Lenny!" scolded Lucy. "Of course not. People like Verloren don't 'fancy' people. They are all class."

IT ONLY TOOK a few months for Verloren and Farkas to establish a pattern that would remain constant throughout their relationship. Verloren knew Farkas did not respect her. That caused her pain. She wanted respect, and even more, she wanted love. It would have been easy if the pain had been unrelenting and unchanging. We leave situations that are constantly painful, or we seriously change them. However, the Greyness is more deceptive than that. It prolongs its lifespan by throwing in occasional light. Those moments of light give us the illusion of hope that we can eventually get what we want from the same scenario. The few moments of tenderness from Farkas fed Verloren. She, in turn, guarded the relationship jealously, believing those moments could become more. She particularly hated it if Maria was mentioned. She would brush off the conversation as boring. If people could kill without going to jail (and perhaps without getting their own hands dirty), they often would. Human nature is like that.

Farkas told himself that it was all about the money. Maria could not help feeling that it was not good for Farkas to have Verloren as such a constant in his life, regardless of how much money it was. Farkas's control of Verloren was less than he imagined. She would undoubtedly work against (even unconsciously) any real improvement in his life. One bit of light leads to another, and it would have led him away from her. The whole thing was the opposite of a healing relationship.

ONE DAY IN THE CAFE, Verloren walked past Maria briskly, and the cups went flying. Verloren didn't apologise or even seem to notice. Maria was upset. Lucy was not a brave person, particularly to someone with as much personal power as Verloren. However, her mother instinct came out.

"Are you alright, Maria?" Lucy asked pointedly.

It was the first time Lucy had even vaguely challenged Verloren.

Verloren quickly turned to Lucy and said, "Oh, I'm sure she's fine. She is much tougher than she looks."

She softened her voice and said, "Poor little Maria. You have had enough challenges, haven't you, dear girl? Why, only the other day, someone said to me, 'Maria has had such a marvellous recovery from her accident, although she has been quite different since the accident. Her parents must wonder if it's even the same person!'"

No one said that to Verloren. She wasn't even sure where it came from. But it came. And she used it. It came with a purpose.

Lucy smiled weakly and said, "Yes, we are lucky."

For some reason, she didn't feel lucky. Her words felt like water dripping through the cracks. The poisonous seed had been planted, and it was already taking root.

Those few sentences from Verloren had the power to change Maria and Lucy's relationship. Lucy couldn't seem to turn the tide. She kept thinking about it, repeating it in her mind, "Her parents must wonder if it's even the same person." The problem was that there was a little too much truth in it, and it wasn't a truth that Lucy could handle.

# CHAPTER 20
# THE SHRINE

The unstated but unmistakable change in Maria's relationship with her mother gave Maria the idea to move out of home. It was a good step, and both spoke positively about it without ever mentioning the underlying reason for the idea. Maria quietly moved out on the arranged day and was living with Charlie, who was thrilled to have her. Charlie had a shed that was occasionally used for visitors, and it was now Maria's home.

Charlie's house was small and, like most artists, cluttered, making it seem even smaller. It had her bedroom, a bedroom for Gabriel (when he was there), and a bedroom that had become the art studio. Gabriel used an old machinery shed for his sculpting studio. That way, he wouldn't be stuck in the house with Charlie for too long.

For cheaper rent, Maria looked after the garden and the animals. She couldn't have been happier with this arrangement and was in her element. How special it is to have a space of one's own when one is used to sharing a house with a family. It feels as luxurious as a palace, even if it is only a shed. The shed had a bed, a little kitchen, and an outside toilet that she shared with the spiders. She had to use the main house for a shower. Everything about it, Maria loved. She wanted her tiny home to be a healing space. Gabriel called it *Maria's Shed*, but Charlie called it *Maria's Shrine* because of the candles, the holy pictures, and how it felt.

Charlie often found reasons to come to the Shrine because she said it felt so nice, and she wanted to escape the clutter in her house and, most likely, the clutter in her mind. Gabriel occasionally came to the door of the Shrine, but he had never been inside. He acted like there was an invisible barrier at the entrance, and while Charlie barged through it, he could not or would not.

SOME MONTHS LATER, Charlie was swearing at the chooks. And the dogs. And anything that moved. Her girlfriend of the past year, Elizabeth, had cheated on her and had confessed to Charlie a few days ago.

"She is having one of her attacks," Gabriel said quietly to Maria while rolling his eyes. "I have to go back to the city now. I will leave you with the crazy woman."

Maria waved goodbye as he drove his car down the long dirt track to the front gate. These days, Maria missed Gabriel when he returned to the city.

"Come on, Charlie," said Maria, trying to break the tension. "It's been three days. You are still acting like a lunatic."

"You bet I am because that daughter of a bitch cheated on me," said Charlie with double the number of expletives as ordinary words.

"I will make you a nice cup of tea, and you can relax here for a while," said Maria, taking her hand and leading her into the Shrine.

Charlie had not visited the Shrine for a few days, which was unusual for her. She thought you couldn't go into the Shrine and swear and fume without feeling ashamed. So, she didn't go there. She was too angry.

Maria spoke to her soothingly, gave her a cup of tea, lit some candles, and let her talk. She talked alright. She talked for an hour nonstop. Maria listened. Over the hour, Charlie's voice gradually became less loud, less furious, and less reckless. As she quietened, she became softer and more open. She started to cry. Then she howled. Maria let her cry for a good ten minutes without hugging her. She didn't want to interrupt the process.

"I know you will tell me not to," said Charlie, "because you are such a goodie-two-shoes, but I hate Elizabeth. I can't help it. I hate her."

"No, you don't," said Maria. "You love her. You are just hurt."

When Charlie had had enough and was ready to return to her own house, Maria told her, "Trust that you will be okay. I know you will be. The whole drama can vanish very quickly if you let it. Talk to Elizabeth without the hate, and try to understand what she is saying and why it happened. You and Elizabeth may be able to salvage the relationship. Mistakes are lessons. And if you can't work it out together, let each other go freely. You loved her once. She is still that same person. Think of that person you once loved. She is that person, whether you are together or not."

## CHAPTER 21
## GENTLE CORRECTOR

Maria didn't walk on the beaches as often nowadays because she had to drive to the back hills, after work, to get home. However, the beach was the place—vast, changing, and unchanging— where she heard Amira's voice most clearly. Today, she was walking and listening.

"You sense that Farkas wishes you no harm and that Verloren does," said Amira, "so you are willing to pray for Farkas but not for Verloren."

Amira was a gentle but direct corrector.

"At this point," said Amira, "that is unacceptable."

Maria wondered who it was "unacceptable" to and what "point" she was at.

"I see," said Maria, who was not sure she saw at all.

"You can turn every ugly and damaging drama into a genuine blessing by seeing it differently," said Amira. "No one is suffering on purpose. We learn to give up the pleasure we feel in self-righteously blaming others. Healing happens when we see things differently. The question is, do you want suffering or peace? It's that simple."

"Hmm," said Maria. "That's a fairly obvious choice, but let me think about it some more!"

"As you wish," said the ever-patient Amira. "Remember, you are not trying to abide the darkness. You are choosing to sit where it is sunny and warm."

LUCY HAD NOT SPOKEN to Lenny about Maria's leaving home or Verloren's comments about her being a different person since the accident. Both were too raw, and she didn't want to give them more power than they already had. This evening, it was time.

"Maria decided to walk on the beach after work today," Lucy told her husband.

"How is she going?" asked Lenny.

"She loves living at Charlie's," said Lucy.

"That's good," said Lenny. "We want her to be happy."

The thought of Maria's happiness opened the door for Lucy.

"Verloren said that people wonder if Maria is the same person since the accident," she said. "What if she isn't our daughter?"

She felt silly saying it, but it felt worse not saying it.

Lenny stopped reading the paper, looked up at the woman he married when he was seventeen, and said, "If we have a daughter with the angels and also a daughter who lives near us, works happily with you every day, and loves us both, then we are very fortunate. We would have two daughters, Lucy, not none."

Lucy looked at her husband of thirty-five years. She felt very blessed, about everything.

THE FOLLOWING WEEKEND, Maria overheard her mother saying to Verloren as she left the cafe, "My daughter decided that she is too old to live at home anymore, but daughters never really leave their mothers."

Verloren stopped walking and looked at Lucy, whose voice was even and forgiving. She didn't hold anything against Verloren. She saw the whole thing as an opportunity for growth and was genuinely happy with her little victory over herself.

"She will always be my daughter," said Lucy, "no matter where she lives, because I will always love her, and it is the love that makes her my daughter."

# BODY

## CHAPTER 22
## FEAR

Charlie and Maria were headed for the Post Office in Waldmeer one lovely, sunny morning. Their sunniness was interrupted by a lone male voice and snickering.

"You still kissin' girls, Charmaine?" said the man-boy.

The intention was to insult. However, Charlie felt it was more insulting to be called Charmaine than about who she was kissing.

"Those idiot boys," she groaned.

Maria knew them well. It was a group of boys from her school year level. She didn't like them then. She still didn't.

*Bullies*, she thought, *led by the biggest bully of all, Harry Maclary.*

Harry's parents owned the dairy outside Waldmeer. He was spoiled, not so much with material things, but with too much pandering and too little responsibility. The result was not pleasant. At school, Harry and his hoon mates often tormented Maria.

*You still a virgin?* they would say to her loudly. *We can help you with that.*

They would then laugh and amble off proudly. Maria was quiet at school and found them embarrassing, offensive, and scary.

Harry was pleased with the annoyed look on Charlie's face and said, "Or you kissin' that pussy-boy you live with?"

The boys found this even funnier. Charlie was no pushover. She had a mouth on her and a spirit to match. However, to Maria's surprise, she withdrew instead of firing up. She remembered that Charlie had recently had more upsetting confrontations with her girlfriend, Elizabeth, and she must have felt defeated. Harry opened his big mouth again as he was on a roll. The other boys looked on with amusement as if it were the best morning fun they had had in a while.

Suddenly, Maria swung around and headed straight for Harry. She disregarded the other boys, who instinctively moved out of the way. Maria had her eyes tunnelling into Harry. He looked startled and tried to regain his position. Every memory of his abusive, threatening behaviour toward her and every other vulnerable girl he had harassed came to the forefront of her mind. His current remarks about Charlie and Gabriel threw fuel onto the fire.

Looking for support, Harry nodded to his boys, who circled Maria and stood a foot above her. Charlie disappeared from view as the tower of boys closed in. She was not afraid—not anymore.

She thought, *You can hurt my body, but I don't care. I will never allow you to hurt my soul ever again. And you will not hurt those I love.*

Maria poked a finger into Harry's chest and said, "Do not

come into our cafe again, Harry Maclary, until you have learned some manners."

Did she say *Harry Maclary*? She might have said *buffoon*. Either way, he got the point. Harry was so shocked that quiet little Maria had lost her fear that he stood there dumbly, and the boys decided to open a path for her to let her out.

When Charlie and Maria got around the corner, they collapsed into laughter. It all seemed so ridiculous, including Maria's reaction.

*IN THE BACK hills of Waldmeer:*

Maria drove up the long driveway to her little shed the following Saturday after work. Gabriel was back for the weekend. He walked up to her car and smiled.

"Charlie told me about your run-in with the buffoon," he said. 'Thank you for defending my 'pussy-boy' status, but you don't need to bother. I am fine."

"Of course, you are fine," said Maria.

"Well, don't put yourself in that position next time," said Gabriel protectively.

*IN WALDMEER:*

A few days later, when visiting the cafe, while Maria was out getting fruit and vegetables, Charlie decided to tell Lucy about the incident with the hoon-boys. Charlie was like that. *Why hide things?* she thought.

That evening, Lucy, in turn, told Lenny. Lucy was a mother. She tended to be understanding of the problems of other people's children. She would say, "There, but for the grace of God, go I," and be thankful that, somehow, she had cornered lots of God's grace.

Lenny said nothing, but he was a father. His job was to protect. Harry and those boys had better watch out the next time they crossed paths with the longtime fisherman of Waldmeer.

A SMALL POSY of flowers was delivered to Waldmeer Corner Store and Cafe a few weeks later, with Maria's name on it. It didn't have a sender's name. It was the sort of posy with pretty pink paper you buy if you don't have a lot of money but want to impress somebody. It had a little handwritten note by someone who looked like they were trying to write neatly but didn't write very often. *Sorry, Maria,* was all it said. The writing looked familiar. A memory from school came up. Maria smiled. She had already forgiven Harry. After all:

*Forgiveness
is something
you give
YOURSELF
every day.*

## CHAPTER 23
## VASTANDAMINE FOREST

I n the back hills of Waldmeer:
One night, around 2.00 a.m., Maria woke and looked out the window of her tiny shed home. The night sky was perfectly clear, with masses of brilliant stars forming a blanket of beauty. Someone was standing next to the bed. Maria was relieved to see that it was Milyaket.

She smiled at Maria and said, "It's lovely seeing you again. How did you go crossing the North Country pass after I left you?"

Maria felt that Milyaket knew precisely how she went, but, to be polite, she said, "Well, I met the wolf pack, and Galahad took me to the border of Garourinn, and there I realised Amira had already returned to me."

"That's wonderful," said Milyaket. "Now, I have somewhere else to take you. Someone is waiting to see you in the Vastandamine Forest in the Homeland."

The Vastandamine Forest is where Farkas met his Earth father.

"If you think so," Maria said hesitantly.

She wondered who would be waiting there for her.

*IN THE INTER-DIMENSIONAL HOMELAND:*

Milyaket took her hand, and before any time seemed to pass, Maria was sitting in the forest, in full daylight, on a grassy patch next to one of the happy rivers dancing along its way. After a few minutes, a man appeared and sat next to her.

"Zufar," said Maria as she hugged and kissed him.

Actually, Maria didn't know who Zufar was. Amira certainly did, although it had been eons since she had seen him.

*LIFETIMES AGO:*

Zufar and Amira were lifelong mates. They fell in love as young adults and were soon married. It was a good, spirited match, and they gave much to each other. Many of their joint life lessons came from their bodies. Sometimes, people love each other and connect in their minds or hearts, but never really connect in their bodies. Zufar was a soldier and strongly aligned with his healthy and strong body. He was also very aligned with Amira's body. They were as much at home with each other's bodies as they were with their own.

In those days, soldiers spent long periods overseas, and many slept with other women while away. Although Zufar did not do this for several years, eventually, he did. Amira knew as soon as he returned. His body was different. Part of it felt foreign. Zufar's guilt made him protect himself. Both decided it was best not to talk about it. They tried to focus on the essence of their love rather than the betrayals to it. They worked to get the purity of their connection back. It took time, but they did get it back. That is, until the next long trip away.

As time progressed, Zufar learned to control his sexual drive rather than it control him. It was a happy day when next he returned home. His body felt as it did when he left home. However, along with Zufar's ability to transcend his body's desires, he also learned to transcend the thought of separate and conflicting bodies in general. He found that he could no longer kill another person. He could not see anyone as an enemy anymore. This was an outstanding achievement as a soul, but a serious conflict as a soldier now in command.

One time, he confronted an enemy to protect one of his men. His soldier escaped. Zufar was unable to harm the enemy and was killed instead. As his guides took him to the Homeland, he told them he was pleased to be going home and no longer wished to live in a world where brothers were seen as enemies. He knew he would see Amira again.

Amira was the one left behind. The grief forced her to learn that souls can never be separated. She could see that even though we have a body that can thrive and be used for beautiful things, it is the changeless soul that connects. After that, she often felt Zufar around and even heard his voice. Her grief was completely healed. Further, the actual capacity for grief was dismantling.

*In the Homeland:*

"It has been a long time," said Zufar.

Amira nodded.

"I have come to tell you," continued Zufar, "that I will be travelling to a different dimension soon, and you will not feel me around for a long time. It is my happy duty to go, but I wanted to let you know."

"My dear, you are so kind to bring me here to say good-bye," said Amira, taking Zufar's hand. "We have already said more goodbyes than are necessary. Those were goodbyes that brought about the end of partings. You have your work, which will bring you great fulfilment, and I have mine. We taught each other that no parting is possible."

Zufar stood up and looked beyond the trees to a distant land.

He turned to Amira, knelt before her and said, "Then, there shall be no parting."

He got up, walked towards the trees, and disappeared.

Maria had been totally voiceless while witnessing Zufar and Amira. She did not know what to say.

"Come," said Amira. "We have work to do and people who need us. It is time to go."

*In the back hills of Waldmeer:*

The stars were no longer shining through Maria's window. The sun was creeping over the hill. The hens were making a racket, and the morning was calling. It was the beginning of a glorious, clear day.

## CHAPTER 24
## A BETTER BOOK

I*n Waldmeer:*

One afternoon, Harry Maclary's twin sister, Mary, entered the cafe. Mary was the opposite of Harry. Reserved, clever, peaceful, polite. An altogether delightful young woman. By now, all three—Harry, Mary, and Maria—were twenty-three.

"I'm so sorry about my brother," said Mary. "You know what he can be like."

She added hopefully, "I'm sure with a few more years, he will work himself out."

"Of course, he will," said Maria, smiling to let Mary know not to give the incident any more thought.

Mary turned to leave but hesitated and quietly said, "Umm, I was wondering if you had a minute?"

"Yes, of course," said Maria.

"I have a problem," said Mary. "And I can't talk to my family about it or anyone else in Waldmeer. They are so conservative."

"Yes," said Maria encouragingly.

"I realised some time ago that I am not attracted to boys," said Mary. "Last time I went to the city, I met a gay girl there, and it dawned on me that I am also gay. There is no one here in Waldmeer that I am interested in. I mean, are there even any gay people in our little town? I just wanted to tell someone who would not repeat what I have said."

Maria smiled and said, "I don't think that's a problem at all. Relationships are valuable no matter who they are between."

Mary looked relieved.

"I think you must come and have dinner at my house," Maria said.

"I'd love to," replied Mary.

"Then come tonight after I finish work," said Maria. "Charlie's property is beautiful, and it will still be light enough for us to walk along Merri Creek."

CHARLIE INSTANTLY LIKED Mary and felt relaxed around her. So relaxed that she soon delved into a deep and honest conversation about Elizabeth. She complained about her girlfriend's numerous infidelities and the almost totally collapsed state of their relationship. Maria let Mary and Charlie do the talking.

"I don't think we have to stay in a repeating bad story," said Mary with calm maturity. "We can pick up a new book that is better and happier just by putting the other book down."

Maria smiled. It was as she thought. Mary was a good match for Charlie, and vice versa. Charlie's life and career were thriving at thirty-five, and she no longer needed to look to other people to make her way. At this stage, it would not matter to her that Mary was younger and only starting her adult life.

In the past, Charlie had always been drawn to women like herself, full of fire. She enjoyed the energy, power, and life force of those relationships. It helped her become who she now was, but they were also full of damaging fireworks. Fire doesn't need more fire. It needs water—calm, healing, restorative water. That was Mary. She was mostly *water,* a substantial bit *earth* for practicality and stability, and a little *air.* Without a little *air,* Mary would not have been able to relate to the creative in Charlie or herself.

*Maybe it's a match made in Heaven,* thought Maria, *but maybe not.*

Relationships are a gift from God. One cannot arrange what is not written in Heaven. Both people must feel the spark of God, which ignites the love and says,

*Come this way. I have a good story for you.*

# BEING SAVED

## CHAPTER 25
## VISITOR

I n *Waldmeer:*
"I'm going to sell my house," Farkas said to Verloren, who was in Waldmeer for the weekend working on her gardening project.

"What?" said a shocked Verloren. "No, I like coming here."

"Then you can buy it," said Farkas.

Verloren liked coming when Farkas was in the house, not when he wasn't. He had already made up his mind about selling, and Verloren did end up buying it. She and her husband would use it as a holiday house.

Farkas knew he needed to go somewhere away from Waldmeer. He didn't know where. However, someone else did know.

∽

IN THE BACK *hills of Waldmeer:*

Maria had just returned from work and settled into her comfy chair. Charlie didn't bother knocking.

"Come and see who came out of the forest today," Charlie said excitedly.

"Is it Erdo?" Maria asked.

She hadn't seen him for quite a while and would love to.

"It's not a *he*," said Charlie, enjoying the suspense.

She pointed to her back door.

"She was ravenous and had a leg injury," said Charlie. "I don't know how long she has been wandering around the forest."

There, on the mat, lay a dog. She was obviously tired, but got on her feet as Maria approached.

"Isn't she a beautiful German shepherd?" said Charlie. "A few days' rest and food, and she will be magnificent."

Maria stopped walking and said, "That's not a German shepherd. It's a wolf."

"Don't be ridiculous," said Charlie. "We don't have wolves in our forest."

Maria and Charlie shared many things, but some things Maria kept to herself. It was not only a wolf but Sage, Galahad's mate, from the North Country. Maria could see from Sage's eyes that she recognised her. Perhaps, Sage even came to find her. She followed Maria back to her shed and, much to Charlie's disappointment, would not leave Maria's side again.

*In Waldmeer:*

Sage refused to be left at home in the mornings and travelled with Maria to Waldmeer Corner Store and Cafe each day. Maria had the uneasy feeling that keeping a wolf as a domestic pet was doomed for failure, but she was so thrilled to have her that she wouldn't allow herself to think about it.

"You stay in the back area," she said to Sage as she headed back into the cafe.

Sage would sit obediently, but sometimes Maria would check on her, and she would be gone. The fences were high. It was a mighty jump, but Sage was used to the wild country up north, and a fence would certainly be no problem. Sage seemed to be scouting for something. When she couldn't find it, she would return to the cafe and try again later. She was agile and adept at keeping a low profile so that no one seemed to notice that there was a wolf in their midst.

One day, Sage was gone longer than usual, and Maria started to worry. Eventually, she returned, but she looked different. She pulled on Maria's hand to open the gate and follow her. She seemed to have found what she was looking for. She took Maria past her parents' house and stopped outside Farkas's. Maria's heart sank. Sage looked calmly into her eyes.

"All right, girl," said Maria, "do as you must."

Farkas was in the process of his final packing, as the Reisendens were taking possession of the house tomorrow. His door was open. Sage went inside with one last backwards glance at Maria. The door closed after her, and Maria slowly walked back down the hill.

*She didn't come for me,* sighed Maria. *She came for Farkas. Oh well. He needs her more than me.*

## CHAPTER 26
## CLOUDS

Farkas recognised Sage immediately. Not only that, but he found he could speak with her as fluently as with a human, probably more so. They headed for the Leleks, crossed Erdo's walking bridge, and began the long walk to the North Country. Farkas had never been on the bridge before. He hesitated a moment, but Sage nudged him on. He now knew where he had to go—back to the pack. He remembered much in the next few weeks of travelling with Sage.

"It will be winter soon in the North Country," he said.

"You will be alright," said Sage. "You can use the abandoned hut. Galahad will get enough supplies for you from the Garden of Garourinn to last the winter. You will remember how to live there once we arrive. We will help you."

*IN THE INTER-DIMENSIONAL NORTH COUNTRY:*

After a quick adjustment, Farkas settled into life in the North Country. For the first time in as long as he could remember, he started to feel genuinely happy and relaxed. He loved the companionship of the wolf pack and the daily life tasks. The harsh conditions did not bother him at all. He had fire, water, and food. The pack would often bring him the kill to take what he wanted first. He did cook it. He could recall much about life in the pack, although he had been a human for a long time. Sometimes, he let the pack stay in the hut overnight, but that was rare. He played with them often and laughed a lot. He found them very funny. They took a lot of pleasure from amusing him, and the play was very healing for Farkas.

One day, close to the end of winter, Farkas went for a long walk over an adjoining mountain. He had not seen the pack that day, which was unusual. After a few hours of walking in soothing, relatively warm sunlight, Farkas was getting hungry. So, he turned for home. He realised he had not noticed the mass of dark clouds fast approaching. It was not good. Once they were upon him, it would be freezing cold and difficult to see anything. He would have to trust his internal compass to get back home.

After half an hour, he was surrounded by cold, swirling darkness and had lost his bearings. He didn't know which direction to walk, and he was still several hours from the hut. Worse, his mind was starting to dissolve into a sea of disturbing images that were getting more intense with every passing minute. Everywhere he looked in the moving darkness were images of past hurts, people he felt had betrayed him, and a mass of sorrows and anger of every imaginable form. It was relentless. Who would think that we could hold so many grievances? Many of the people he could not even recognise. But they contributed to the throbbing, grey beast now hunting him from every angle.

Farkas found a ledge and sat under it, trying to protect himself from the bitter wind. He wouldn't survive long if he just sat there, but he did not want to go back into the tormenting gloom. He could neither defeat it nor even understand it. The image of a man appeared to his right. Farkas thought it was another of the tormenting images, and he shuddered closer to the rock face. He tried to brush it aside, but it wouldn't move.

"I see you have returned," said the stranger.

The other images were voiceless. This one talked.

"We have met before," the man continued. "You once saved my youngest child and paid for it with your own life. I gave you a different life—a human one."

Now, Farkas knew who it was. It was the Head Gardener from the Garden of Garourinn. He jumped to his feet out of relief and respect.

"We will walk together. You are not alone, but you must do as I ask," said the Head Gardener, who had already turned into the multitude of gruelling images.

"I don't want to go back out there," said Farkas.

"It is the only way for you to get back home," said the Head Gardener. "All these images are of your own making. You made them, and your anger feeds them and keeps them alive. You have given them all the power that they have. Walk through them, and they will leave. I cannot do that for you, but I can show you which direction to walk. You must do the walking yourself. Let us go, or it will be night before we reach the end of them."

Farkas did as the Head Gardener asked. He only slightly believed that it would work. However, as he squarely looked at each image and walked through it, it disintegrated. It was, however, immediately replaced with another harrowing image. As he kept walking, he became more confident in the process. He felt he was getting somewhere and detected a tiny bit of light in the blackness. Eventually, the conglomeration of images seemed to be thinning. Relieved and exhausted, he could see his home mountain in the distance. A small moving blur was heading from the mountain to where he was walking. It was the pack.

"I must return to the Garden now," said the Head Gardener. "Remember, Farkas, every grievance you hold hides a little more of the world's light from your eyes until the darkness becomes overwhelming. Everything you forgive restores that light. So, ask yourself, who is it that you are really hurting?"

## CHAPTER 27
## SPECIAL

*In Waldmeer:*

It was a sad time for Verloren. Farkas's house had a quick settlement, and she was soon unlocking the door with her key instead of knocking on the door and Farkas opening it for her. Despite his ambivalence towards and sometimes abuse of her, Verloren would miss him greatly over the coming months. It was a childish and irrational wish to want Farkas to love her, but don't we all do this?

We make people special to us, believing that they can save us. Verloren was perhaps more obvious in her quest, less reserved than others, and more aggressive in what she wanted. But who could blame her for doing something we all do, even if others do it with more grace? It's still the same idea of believing someone else can save us from ourselves.

With time, Verloren would probably transfer that longing to another person with a version of the same results. Don't we do that too? When one thing doesn't work, we look elsewhere to be saved. We rarely question the concept itself.

Sometimes, we don't look to another person to save us, but to money, acknowledgement, a title, a cause, or a notion of ourselves. None of it can save us. We travel the path differently; some are more polite, some are ruthless, some are clever, and some are instinctive. In the end, it all leads to the same despairing place.

Amid all this searching and not finding, Verloren was given a special gift. She now had a house in Waldmeer, which had healing energy capable of helping people if they would let it. In the unsuspecting quiet moments, there it was, bringing in a sense of peace and a feeling that everything was fine without searching for anything to be saved by. It softened the grabbing for love and the blaming when that stupid grabbing didn't work.

One evening, while walking back to her newly acquired house in the fading light, Verloren remembered a dream she once had. In the dream, her grandfather told her how to get to the Garden of Garourinn. A person called the Head Gardener suggested she revisit it in her sleep. She had the dream a long time ago. In all that time, Verloren had not even thought about it once. That night, a thought crossed her mind as she lay her head on the pillow and drifted off to sleep while listening to the faint waves in the distance.

*I might be able to find the Garden of Garourinn in my dreams,* she thought.

She was, at last, looking in a place that could actually help her.

# NEW BEGINNING

# CHAPTER 28
# MOVING

*In the back hills of Waldmeer:*
One weekend, in late winter, everyone sat on Charlie's veranda listening to the early evening sounds and Gabriel's idea. His living arrangement in the city had changed, and he had found a large, rambling house in one of the alternative inner-city suburbs. He proposed that everyone move there— he, Maria, Charlie, and Mary.

"It has three big bedrooms," said Gabriel. "One for me, one for Maria, and one for Charlie and Mary."

Since Mary first visited Charlie's property, she and Charlie had become inseparable. Elizabeth was long gone. Mary had an excellent effect on Charlie, who now had a calmness that had been absent before, adding to her already successful direction.

"Mary wants to start her university studies," Gabriel continued, "and Charlie has so many offers in the city that she could spend all week responding to them. The house has a workshop at the back, which Charlie and I can share, and a shop front which we can use as a gallery. There is a closed-in side veranda which I think Maria should use. She could start to see people and help them."

"How?" asked Maria.

"I don't know," said Gabriel, frustrated by the question. "How would I know? You will work it out once we get there. Turn it into a *Shrine*. You know how much Charlie loves going into your *Shrine* here. If she likes it, other people will too."

He said it as if only people like Charlie would want to go into it, not people like him. However, he was the one who thought up the idea. So, he can't have been that dissociated from it.

Everyone just nodded, and that was that. They were moving. Charlie went to the local Waldmeer real estate and told them she would rent her property. The rent would pay her mortgage for now. That way, she wasn't completely cutting her ties with Waldmeer.

## CHAPTER 29
## CANDLES

I n *the back hills of Waldmeer:*
  Maria closed the door of her shed one last time. There was no lock on it. There had never been. She realised she had left two pictures and several half-used candles on the windowsill. For some reason, she decided to leave them there, although she had been told to completely empty the shed for the future renters.

"Goodbye, my dear home," she said to the Shrine. "You have loved me, so I leave part of myself here with you."

BY EARLY SPRING, Farkas was back in Waldmeer. There was not much to rent, so he took Charlie's property. The isolated location suited him after the North Country mountains. To help with the rent, he decided to rent out Maria's old shed. However, each time he called into the real estate agent to let them know, he got to the desk, made some excuse, and walked out again.

*I'll do it another day*, he kept telling himself.

Farkas noticed the shed door had blown open one morning after a storm. When he went to close it, he saw something on the windowsill.

*Maria has left some of her stuff behind*, he thought.

He sat on the bare floor and listened. Not for anything in particular. It was calm and still after the storm. He got up, lit one of the candles, and sat down again.

*It's Maria*, Farkas said to himself. *I can feel Maria is here. It must be that candle. She always was a strange girl.*

It was Amira more than Maria, but Farkas could not distinguish them. Nor did he even know Amira's name. He only knew Maria, who was now gone. Farkas sat there a long time. He didn't move.

"I'm sorry," he eventually said.

Farkas wasn't a man to say sorry. There would have been too much to say sorry for.

*You did well,* said the candle.

It sounded like Maria's voice, but older. More distant, but also very close.

"You were brave to come anywhere near me," said the voice. "At some level, you knew that every thought you cherished would be taken apart, every grudge you harboured would be thrown back at you, and every ancient dream you held would be put into the fire."

Farkas didn't say anything. He was a little pleased that he could hear the voice. He knew it was a gift but also an earned right.

"It is not just desperation that does that," continued the voice. "It is a belief in oneself, that one can do better, that one is worth it."

After a bit, Farkas got up and blew the candle out. If he

wanted to speak to Maria again, she might come back if he lit one of the half-used candles. He wanted to save them. Opening the door of the little shed, he smelled the sweet freshness after the storm. Maria's words went with him as he walked out into the day.

# PART II
# IN ERALDUS

## THE DIVIDING LINE

# THE CITY

# CHAPTER 30
# MONEY

I n Eraldus:

Gabriel sat down on Maria's bed as he had done many times in the city house, which they were now sharing with Charlie and Mary in Eraldus.

"I know you are trying your best, but you need to earn more money," said Gabriel. "Our first six-month lease is up, and they are increasing our rent."

As suggested back in Waldmeer, Maria set up the veranda as a healing space. It wasn't lacking clients. Most days, people knocked on the house door asking for the healing girl. She listened to their problems and helped them as much as she could.

"You have lots of clients, and they love you," said Gabriel. "You should be making lots of money by now."

He paused and thought he sounded too materialistic.

"I just don't understand it. That's all. I never see you buying anything for yourself. Where does your money go?"

Maria had not explained to him that her spirit counterpart, Amira, had told her that she was not to charge any money for healing. She was allowed to have a donation box. Many of the people who came had less money than Maria or had children and more urgent needs. She didn't want to take their money. Those who had money didn't necessarily give it. Generally, those with no money insisted on giving the most. Maria felt that what was freely given to her by the spirit world must be freely shared with others, although that was not right for everyone. Otherwise, no one would be making any money.

Without mentioning Amira, Maria explained the donation box to Gabriel. She already knew what the response would be.

"Please don't worry about me. I have enough for our rent and bills, and I am fine," she said.

Later that evening, Maria told Charlie what Gabriel had been saying to her.

"He said not to tell you," said Charlie, "but you haven't been paying your full share of the rent for the past six months. He has been adding to your share to make it equal to ours. He said it would give you a chance to get on your feet financially. Otherwise, the rent would be too much for you. Now, the rent is going up, and he thinks you still aren't able to pay the first amount, let alone the new amount."

"Oh, I see," said Maria.

It is one thing to make choices about one's lifestyle and quite another to be a burden on someone else.

*It isn't just the money,* thought Gabriel as he worked on one of his sculpture projects in the workshop. *Maria has become quite spacey and ungrounded since living in the city.*

He didn't know if it was the effect of all the troubled people she was seeing, if it was living in the city that didn't agree with her, or if it was living with him, Charlie, and

Mary. He felt that putting her mind to the practical task of making money would bring her back into a more functional space.

The next day, he overheard the manager at their local cafe say she was looking for staff. He told her about Maria's experience in her mother's cafe in Waldmeer. The manager already knew Maria from coming to the cafe, and she liked her from day one. She liked all the residents of their house.

"Of course, we'll take her. She can have a shift tomorrow as someone is sick," said the manager.

"Thank you for finding me a proper job," Maria said to Gabriel somewhat apologetically. "I will start tomorrow."

The issue seemed resolved, and both put the minor upset out of their minds. Little did they realise it was the forerunner of a real fight.

# CHAPTER 31
# SEEING SOULS

Maria would often see the souls of people around her. Although some souls were more invisible, most were obvious, and some were transparently clear. She had to remind herself that other people could generally not see the same thing, and so they didn't have the same information as she did.

She did not see souls visually, although they may have elements that were relayed visually. It was a *knowing* something to be true. It was the transfer of information, usually not specific or detailed information. It was the general state of the person, the stage that the soul was at developmentally, and the issues they were working on.

If someone had a life-threatening illness or a serious accident, not infrequently, Maria would know if it was their time to go or not. If someone had suicidal thoughts, she would often sense the seriousness of the situation, pray for them, and sometimes do something else.

Not infrequently, she could feel the presence of those who had recently died around their loved ones. Dead mothers, in particular, seemed to love her. Of course, no one is really dead, and that is the irony. Maria had little, if any, control over what she did or didn't see.

Six months after her accident as a teenager, she had an experience of a relative's death, which taught her an invaluable lesson. One of her great-aunts was very ill, and everyone knew that death was near. The great aunt's sister had asked Maria to visit the dying woman. Maria didn't go. Not long after the funeral, the great-aunt chastised Maria for not going to see her sister, as requested.

Maria was surprised and said, "Aunty, why are you angry with me?"

"You didn't go and say goodbye to her, and now it's too late," said the great-aunt.

Still confused, Maria said, "But none of it matters now."

She meant that it would not matter to the deceased great-aunt. Now that she had passed, she would realise how unbreakable the ties of love are and that no one had gone anywhere. Understandably, her great-aunt did not appreciate Maria's response and looked at her as if she must be terribly mean. What a mismatch of communication lines.

After that, Maria always reminded herself that normal people think deceased people have gone away, perhaps even disintegrated entirely. She mustn't say things that seem mean when she was simply unconcerned because there was nothing to be concerned about.

## CHAPTER 32
## PURPOSE

Although Maria started work at the cafe with the best intentions, it wasn't going very well. The manager and staff were kind to her, and Maria was very fond of them, but she was having trouble concentrating. She found it difficult to remember the relentless series of left-brained tasks.

One of the problems was Maria's ability to see people's souls. She would get distracted by the many things she saw around the customers and find it hard to concentrate on the practical tasks. The customers seemed to sense her interest, maybe because she couldn't help staring at some of them, and they frequently took the opportunity to tell her about their problems. However, this was a cafe, not a healing room. The queue of tasks would get longer. The manager was unusually patient with Maria, but the problem remained.

Back in Waldmeer Corner Store and Cafe, Maria's mother had a far more grounding effect on her than either of them had realised. If Maria were too dreamy, her mother would pull her back to practical issues, and Maria always obliged. Being mother and daughter, much was communicated non-verbally. Lucy also knew when to leave her alone. If she was absorbed in a conversation with a customer, Lucy knew it would be because that person needed her daughter, so she would make things work around that. She gave her a lot of leeway because she trusted her daughter's intentions. It was a good balance, and it worked. The town of Waldmeer itself added to its working because its spiritual energy protected Maria, whereas the city's energy mostly seemed to do the opposite.

Two little blonde sisters, four and five, often came into the city cafe with their parents. No one liked them, which is an uncustomary response to children. They were loud, obnoxious, and spoiled. They were somewhat better with their father, but they were ugly when their mother was present. It wasn't that their mother didn't care about them. She talked to them constantly, read, played with them, and bought them treats and whatever else they wanted. She was intelligent and polite, so she tried to correct their lack of manners, but her pitiful pleas fell on deaf ears. Maria felt sorry for them all.

When their mother wasn't looking, Maria sometimes stared at the girls fiercely so they knew to behave better. The girls hated it, but because she also smiled at them whenever she had the chance, they didn't avoid her.

"I don't know what to do," said the mother to Maria one afternoon as she brought her coffee. "The girls are not at school yet, and I have so much work to do, and every nanny leaves."

The mother was very good at her work and felt much more affirmed in that environment than in her failing child-raising one. The little sisters, Marilyn and Bianca, were squabbling over their cakes, getting louder by the second. Suddenly, the younger one stopped fighting as if her mother's conversation had registered in her mind.

"I know, Mummy. Maria can look after us," said Bianca.

Everyone was surprised, but no one said no. They were all silent and stared at Maria. Even the cafe manager, who heard the conversation, had stopped moving. Everyone was waiting.

Maria turned to the manager and asked, "Would it be all right?"

The manager tried not to look too thrilled and said, "We will miss you, but if they need you, then we will manage."

She turned towards the kitchen and breathed out with a relieved smile.

Maria looked at the children, who were still strangely silent.

"Alright, but we are all going to behave. Everyone is going to be good," she said firmly.

Maria needed a work purpose other than making money. The family truly needed her, and that made all the difference. The mother couldn't have looked happier, and the family walked out of the cafe as if they were walking out of a fog.

# TRUST

## CHAPTER 33
## NOTHING

Right from the start, Paul didn't like Maria. She had nothing against him, but we are careful with people who dislike us. Gabriel had many gay friends in the city. It was a part of his life that Maria had no contact with until they were housemates. Now, she met some of those friends when they visited the house. One of them was Paul.

Maria was sitting in the back courtyard in a bit of afternoon sunshine that had forced its way through the surrounding buildings. She heard Gabriel and Paul walking from the house and was about to make her presence known when Paul stopped walking.

"Why is that girl from the country living here?" said Paul.

"She's just a housemate," said Gabriel.

Something in Gabriel's voice surprised Maria.

*Just a housemate,* she repeated. *I thought we were friends.*

"She seems a bit strange to me," said Paul. "And she has that room at the side of the house. What's that all about?"

"I don't know," said Gabriel, getting edgy. "It's nothing to do with me."

*Nothing to do with me?* thought Maria.

"You seem very buddy-buddy with her," probed Paul, not yet satisfied with the response.

"Nah, bro. I already told you," said Gabriel. "She just lives here. What she does or doesn't do is no interest to me."

Paul took a few more steps, and Maria and Gabriel faced each other. She did not try to hide the look of hurt on her face.

Gabriel looked mortified but quickly regained his composure and said, "Oh, hi Maria, we are just on our way out."

Paul looked neither surprised to see Maria nor sorry about anything said.

That evening, Maria saw Gabriel in the hallway.

"Have you finished with the bathroom?" he asked.

"Yes, I have," said Maria.

However, she didn't move from the doorway, so Gabriel had to look at her.

"I'm not homophobic, but some of your friends are heterophobic," she said.

"Don't worry about it, Maria. It's nothing," said Gabriel.

"You mean *nothing* like I am to you?" asked Maria.

"I don't care how body appendages and holes relate to each other," she said with uncharacteristic bluntness.

"That's not very nice," interrupted Gabriel.

It wasn't clear if he thought it wasn't nice to talk about body appendages and holes or if it wasn't nice to talk about his friends like that.

"You lot have made an invisible club," said Maria, "and if anyone questions its tenets, the brotherhood turns on them.

You all have token women as if to prove how well-adjusted you are. They might as well be trophy wives. You don't want to be equal. You want to be exclusive and special. You are no more special than anyone else."

Gabriel turned for downstairs, and Maria heard the front door bang.

# CHAPTER 34
# MAGIC MIST

Early next morning, Maria was sitting on the bus to Waldmeer, staring out the window. The bus was weaving its way around the endless coastal curves. She opened the window slightly, even though the morning air was cold, and breathed in the fresh saltiness as if it were an all-purpose remedy. Mist rose from the ocean in uneven clouds, hit the surrounding green hills, and then settled back to form a blanket of translucent magic that hovered above the water.

None of the four of them had returned to Waldmeer since their departure six months ago. Charlie, and therefore Gabriel, no longer had a house to return to. Of course, Maria and Mary had family in Waldmeer. Maria's parents belonged to a long line of Waldmeer dwellers. Mary's parents owned the local dairy. Along with Mary's twin brother, Harry, the girls had been school peers since they were children. They missed Waldmeer deeply, and it was for this reason that they had not been home. They had Waldmeer in their blood. They were born and fed on its invisible energy. Living in the city was a marked contrast. If they had returned too soon, they might not have gotten back on the bus to the city, although Charlie would have come looking for Mary.

Maria had left a note for Gabriel, Charlie, and Mary on the kitchen table when she left in the dark at 5 a.m. She explained that the children she minded, Marilyn and Bianca, would be away with their parents, and Maria's mother said she could use some help in Waldmeer Corner Store and Cafe.

The rhythmic movement of the bus and the continuous rolling of the sea had a calming effect on Maria as it did on everyone. She didn't exactly regret what she said to Gabriel. There was a lot of truth in it. Besides, some things need to be said. However, she had been in the spiritual slipstream too long to fool herself that what she said was the real issue. It was not her calling to challenge the gay community. Its problems would not have made her that upset. However, Gabriel's dismissal of her would have. Anger is a cover for fear.

It was almost 8.00 a.m., and Maria could see her little hometown in the distance as the bus rounded the last of the coastal bends. She stepped from the bus as if re-entering a curious and irresistible world and headed to the cafe to start work for the day.

## CHAPTER 35
## SAFETY

Each day after work, Maria roamed the beach before trekking up the big hill to her parents' cottage. Wind, silence, waves, far sea—it was all beautiful. She wanted the conflict to bless her and not leave its mark without its benefit.

"Why are you being so dramatic?" asked Amira, whose voice had no static on the beach.

"I don't have many friends," said Maria. "The ones I do have are important to me."

Her few friends were carefully chosen, although not exactly chosen by her. She faltered as if searching for that point in the centre of a problem from which all the pain radiates. We must be brave enough to pull the simple, biting answer from the depths of our murky consciousness.

Maria saw a spurt of water in the ocean and knew a mother whale and her calf were out there. During winter and early spring, Waldmeer became a calving ground. Like other herd mammals, pregnant whales often isolate themselves and go to a safe place to give birth. The high swells, surrounding cliffs, and deep waters protected them from predators.

"If Gabriel feels pressured by other people," said Maria, "he will retreat into doing whatever seems least stressful and confrontational. He will not protect me."

She looked out to the mother whale, who was now playing with her calf, breaching and catching the sunlight on her massive, wet body.

"You are being too harsh," said Amira after a while. "You have been on the path a long time. You cannot expect Gabriel to know everything you know. It is only when we are far enough along to realise the sorry state most people are in that we lose our concern with what other people think of us."

The whales were quiet now. The sea was still as the gentle glow of dusk began pulling itself over the settling giant.

"It takes courage to tread one's course," said Amira, "but only at the beginning of each new stage. We hope that we are safe, but we are not yet sure. Go back to Eraldus. There is nothing to be angry about and nothing to fear."

Eraldus means *the dividing line.* Maria sometimes wondered what the dividing line was between. She would soon find out.

# LANEWAYS

# CHAPTER 36
# BLOODLINES

Being an older, inner-city suburb, Eraldus had many laneways crisscrossing behind the houses. Maria often walked them because they were much quieter than the streets. They were paved with uneven cobblestones and marked with weeds, puddles, graffiti, and solitude. Eraldus was originally a Greek area, and many olive trees and vegetable gardens were growing over and through the back fences. In marked contrast to the stunning beauty of the Waldmeer beaches, the laneways were a vacuum. There was little to look at, and so one started looking inwards. The energy in the laneways was different from that of the surrounding suburb. For one thing, Amira's voice was particularly clear. However, other voices of lesser realms also seemed to make their presence known up and down the empty pathways.

It was a cloudy, cool afternoon with only occasional rays of sunlight. The laneways were quiet as usual, yet Maria kept feeling that they were poised on the verge of action. Several times, she turned a corner and thought she saw the fleeting movements of a group of dogs in the distance. That was strange because there were no stray dogs in Eraldus. Maria stopped walking. Something was there. She couldn't see anything but decided to head to the nearest street and get out of the lanes. A woman came from the shadows and stood in the lane ahead of Maria.

*Perhaps, it is one of the elderly Greek women,* thought Maria.

As Maria passed, the woman said, "Why are you running away from me? I am your Great Aunt Evanora."

*Evanora?* thought Maria.

Yes, she had a great-aunt called Evanora. It was one of the sisters of the great-aunt who died when Maria was sixteen. It was her father's side of the family. Maria only occasionally saw some of the sisters and had the impression that they were a strange mix, ranging from very good to very bad. But which was Evanora? Evanora looked at Maria with eyes that were both vacant and full of vengeance. She pulled a gun from her coat and took aim. Just as Maria felt she could not save herself, a great wind pushed her over, and she heard a thunder of growls. She barely dared to look at the horrible attack on Evanora by the wolves. It was Galahad and part of his pack, about six male wolves, from the North Country. Although extremely relieved to be rescued, it was a deeply distressing sight. She sat motionless, unable to speak.

"Do not worry," said Galahad. "We have not killed Evanora. We have only destroyed her temporary form so she realises we are watching over you."

Sure enough, in a few moments, the bloodied remains of Evanora started to disintegrate and completely disappeared.

"Would the bullet have killed me? Was it real?" asked Maria.

"Your belief in its reality gave it some power, so we did

not want to take that risk," said Galahad. "One day, you will realise that the bullet and Evanora have no power whatsoever to hurt you."

"Will she come back?" asked Maria.

"Not for now," said Galahad. "We are the guardians of your spiritual bloodline."

"Do you mean my family?" asked Maria.

"No," said Galahad. "Some members of your spiritual bloodline have been in your family. Sometimes, there has been no one in it for generations. Other times, there have been several people in it at once. Whenever the light is strongest, there is also darkness."

"What about my great aunts?" asked Maria.

"As you know, there were four sisters in that family grouping," said Galahad. "One was the aunt who died. Another was the aunt who was upset with you for not visiting before the sister's passing. Then there was Evanora. You cannot remember seeing her when she was alive. She was sent into your bloodline to prevent the spiritual light of the last-born sister, Rose. Evanora watched her youngest sister relentlessly because she hated the light, and hated Rose."

"What happened to the light sister?" asked Maria.

"She lived elsewhere," said Galahad, "and only recently transitioned to the Homeland."

Galahad moved swiftly with his pack to the end of the lane and disappeared.

## CHAPTER 37
## LETTER

A few weeks after the laneway experience, Maria sat at the table with Gabriel, Charlie, and Mary. Strangely, they were all there at the same time for dinner, which rarely happened. Maria was opening a letter she had received. It was the only letter she would ever receive in that house. She read it out loud.

> We want to advise you that your great aunt, Rose Este, has bequeathed her property to you at 6 Mir St, Eraldus. Once the legal documents have been signed, you will have sole ownership of the house.

Everyone was as shocked as Maria. They worked out that it was only a few streets away, so they walked there excitedly. The house was dark and covered with overgrown bushes. The vines had grown up the front of the house, made their home in the accumulated soil in the gutters, and were happily spreading out over the roof. No one could have lived there for some time. The front gate had a tree trunk strewn across it, making it impossible to open. They climbed over the gate, pushed through the bushes, and made their way to the front door. It was one of the original little council-owned houses in the area. Maria loved it instantly.

It was only a matter of a few months, and Maria had possession of the house, had done elementary repairs, and was moving in. Every day she worked there, Amira talked to her. Maria wondered whether this was Amira's house more than hers. Amira told her that although she had two bedrooms, she shouldn't let anyone else live there. She was to use the spare bedroom as her healing room. Maria didn't know how to explain to her housemates that she couldn't share her house with any of them. She wasn't even sure why Amira wanted her to live there alone. In the end, she said little except that she was only a few streets away. Gabriel's friend, Paul, took Maria's room.

Maria was no longer a girl. She was a young woman with a house, a business, and a purpose. Yet, the child in us remains. It lives in our weaknesses. It lives in our trust. It lives in our desire to hold another's hand. It lives in our devotion to something bigger than ourselves.

# CHAPTER 38
# RETREAT

For the next few months, Maria went into an unintended but not unwelcome retreat. There was a lot of practical work to patiently attend to in the house. That kept her semi-focused on the material world. And she still had the children to mind. The care of two little girls also helped to keep her grounded. She saw her clients, but much of that time was spent in a healing consciousness. Apart from the children and her clients, she spoke to almost no one for the coming months. No one in this domain, anyway. She felt the house itself needed healing or enlivening. Her Great Aunt Rose would come and go, in spirit form, as if to check the progress of the house. Perhaps it was to check the progress of Maria.

Her healing room looked beautiful with little effort. It had a massage table where people could relax while Maria put her hands on them and prayed. They often fell asleep. The room had a soft light that seemed to say, *Relax, relax, everything is fine.* The scented candles flickered and filled the room with loveliness. Although Maria had not yet resurrected the garden, she found rose bushes under the rubbish. Most days, a little vase of roses sat on her table, reminding all that the world has such beauty. During this period, Maria became strangely unaware of her body. Yet, it functioned better than ever before. Usually, people have minor complaints about their bodies most of the time, if not major ones. Yet, her body seemed to have none. She often forgot about it entirely, and it seemed to forget about her.

The primary focus of her thought was forgiveness. It wasn't the forgiveness of trying to be nice to nasty people. That becomes passive-aggression or, at best, repression. It wasn't the forgiveness that says, *Even though you have done this, I will overlook it because I am better than you.* No, it was the forgiveness that alters our perception. It sees the spiritual truth and loses sight of the alternatives. Our ego refuses to do this because its main food is remembering the wrongdoings against us, even if they are entirely fabricated. To choose to see a different reality leaves the ego no room. It is the healing space. It is the beautiful space. It is the space of love and happiness.

Maria would not be left too long in her retreat, or it may become permanent. The hand of life would soon be knocking on her door, requiring her return.

# MIR STREET

## CHAPTER 39
## BROKEN

Gavin was one of those good people who fixed up broken highchairs, broken families, and broken dogs. Semi-retired, all-round handyman, a little gruff as men that age often are, but sweet inside. He was one of Maria's Mir Street neighbours, along with his two dogs, whom he was tough on but adored—the perfect dog owner.

"Would you come with me to the pound?" asked Maria one morning as she walked past his house. "I have seen a dog there that interests me, but I need a second opinion. If you say no, then I won't get him."

WHEN THEY ENTERED THE POUND, Maria said, "By the way, he won't let anyone touch him."

Gavin frowned. He had a duty of care to give appropriate advice.

"What breed of dog?" he asked.

"German shepherd," said Maria, keeping up the casual style.

"An aggressive German shepherd?" said Gavin, as if he wasn't going to waste his time by going any further.

"Please, at least, look at him," said Maria. "They won't keep him any longer."

They both stood outside his cage. The dog certainly knew they were there, but he would not do them the honour of looking at either. He was matted and dirty because he wouldn't let the groomer touch him.

"He's way too big for you," said Gavin. "He will hurt you. Have a look at the other dogs. There are lots here that need a good home."

*He would be a fine dog if he stopped fighting life,* thought Gavin.

"His spirit isn't broken, but his trust is," said Gavin.

After Gavin left, Maria sat by the dog's door, waiting for him to show interest in her.

*Gavin didn't exactly say no,* thought Maria.

"Come on, boy," she said. "I'm your only chance. Take it. I'm on your side, but I won't force you. It is your choice for life or not. You will have to let me put the lead on if you are going to get out of this place alive."

The dog listened intently but suspiciously. Maria had been sitting on the floor waiting so long that she started daydreaming. She was surprised by a nose in her hand.

*Thank God,* she thought.

As she slowly clipped the lead to his collar, he suddenly bit her arm. A German shepherd bite is no little scratch. They can kill if they want to.

One of the pound keepers approached and asked, "Is everything alright?"

Maria quickly pulled her jumper over her arm and said, "All good, thanks."

This time, the dog let Maria attach his lead, and they walked to the office. She knew taking a dog that could attack was a great risk. What if he attacked someone else? Yet, she also knew he wasn't bad, just broken.

Maria named him Gortaithe, which means injured in Irish. Sensing the risk she took to save him, he never again challenged her. He quickly gained a reason to live other than self-preservation. When we love someone, we make it our business to protect them.

## CHAPTER 40
## STEALING OR HEALING

"Hello, Verloren," said Maria, with surprise, as she opened her front door.

Maria was used to calling her Mrs Reisenden over the years of seeing her at Waldmeer Corner Store and Cafe, but she was too old to call her that now.

"I hope you don't mind me coming unannounced," said Verloren. "Your mother gave me your new address."

"It's fine. Come in," said Maria.

Verloren eyed the peeling paint on the walls and the bare, unpolished floorboards in Maria's lounge room. She turned her gaze to Maria and smiled.

"Your mother told me about your healing work," she said. "You probably don't know that I have a great interest in such things."

Maria was not so sure that the "such things" they were interested in were the same "such things", but she listened attentively.

"I would like to purchase a healing session," said Verloren.

"I see," said Maria. "What is it that you want healing for?"

"I didn't realise that one had to give a reason for wanting a healing," said Verloren, "but I am having a little issue with Farkas from Waldmeer. You remember him?"

"Yes, of course," said Maria.

"We had something of a falling out," said Verloren. "I am not one to hold a grudge, but I have recently seen him a few times in Waldmeer with a new female companion. It has come to my attention that he is moving forward, and as I have no other option, I need to set a few things right."

Maria knew Verloren was nowhere near ready to accept any true healing at this stage. Not only would it not work, but she would take whatever energy she could from Maria and use it against her at some future point. Further, Verloren's anger at seeing Farkas with a prospective partner would have ignited growing vindictiveness. *Hell hath no fury like a woman scorned.*

"I don't do healings on people unless I have worked with them for a while," said Maria.

Never one to accept *no* for an answer, Verloren said, "What is it that you would like to know?"

"Can you tell me why the falling out with Farkas is painful to you?" asked Maria.

For one brief moment, Verloren's face opened up like a window. There was no doubt her pain was substantial.

"I just wanted him to love me. Was that too much to ask?" she said.

Although she felt sorry for Verloren, Maria also knew she had much resilience in the face of pain and perseverance in trying to get what she wanted. Verloren needed a brutal awakening because nothing else would work.

"Yes, it was," said Maria. "It was way too much. Many women like Farkas. Why do you think he should love you over other women? Are you more beautiful, talented, accomplished, loving or wise? What were you going to give him that he actually wanted?"

Verloren was taken aback and scrambled for an answer, but couldn't think quickly enough to find one. She was smart, but truth is smarter.

"You are being delusional," continued Maria. "I am not saying this to hurt you, but to help you. If you cannot face the obvious facts of the situation, you will never be able to move on to the deeper issues."

Verloren had already stopped listening. She was too angry. It is very confronting to be faced with our most treasured delusions.

She forced a smile and said as calmly as she could muster, "You are wrong, Maria. We were very close. He loved me. He just couldn't tell me, and now he has decided to look for someone else."

"You weren't close," said Maria. "He didn't love you. He used you for money."

Verloren was furious, but she pulled herself together, remembering the other issue she had come to see Maria about.

"You are entitled to your opinion," said Verloren, "but before I go, there is one other issue that I wanted to mention. I had a professional arrangement with Farkas about his garden, and he has not fulfilled his part properly. I was willing to let it slide in the hope that he would come good, but I believe there is little hope of that now. So I will be forced to use legal channels to right the wrong done to me."

She paused and added, "I don't normally repeat things,

but I will tell you, in confidence, that he has said many bad things about you."

"Well, I'm sure he didn't mean them," said Maria.

Verloren stood up to leave and slid her expensive shoe along the rough floorboards.

"You look like you could use a little help restoring your house," she said.

"I like it like this," said Maria, walking Verloren to the door.

*I can lie too,* she thought.

## CHAPTER 41
## INEVITABLE BUT NOT NECESSARY

That evening, Maria sat at the kitchen table with a cup of tea.

"I can't stand her," she said to Amira. "She's so damaging."

"Verloren is damaging because, like most people, she is damaged," said Amira.

Unlike Maria, Amira was never angry. She forgave everyone because she loved everyone equally. No matter what anyone did, she treated them like misguided children. Because of their problems, they were more to be loved and helped.

"The issue is not Verloren," said Amira. "It is your consciousness. Look at yourself. You are all worked up and keep rerunning the scenario in your mind, getting nowhere. Wouldn't you like to get your peace back? Wouldn't you like to feel happy again? Is the self-righteous anger worth it?"

&#8766;

IN TIME, Verloren would return. Time is not necessary for healing, but it is inevitable.

We find many friends when we are down and out. People swarm around with proclamations of, "Oh, how dreadful. How terrible."

They may as well say, "Thank you so much for making me feel better about myself and my life. You have more problems than I and are more pathetic."

Yet, when we enter the healing path, few will be standing there to wish us well, in case we find it.

MARIA OPENED the back door and looked into the clear, cold night. The moon was shining between the houses on its way into its rightful nightly place. She got ready for bed and listened as she lay her head on the pillow. The house was very still. The darkness was inviting and comforting, like a warm blanket.

She closed her eyes and said to the angels, "Take me somewhere beautiful tonight and teach me something wonderful. When I wake up, I will be happy and ready to share my happiness with anyone who would like it."

The darkness fell more deeply over her, and then the Light silently moved in.

# CHAPTER 42
# KISSING

*everal weeks later:*
    The man bent over Maria and kissed her softly on the lips. He didn't wait long and kissed her again. It felt so nice. Warm and sharing. He wasn't taking anything, sucking the life out of her. He was joining with her, whole, unburdened. She slowly opened her eyes to look at his face. The early morning light was filtering under the curtain.

*That's what kissing really is,* thought Maria. *I don't care if it was a dream. It was a good one.*

"Do you remember the Jamiesons, the retired couple who came to live in Waldmeer a few years ago?" Maria's mother asked her on the phone that morning.

"Yes, why?" said Maria.

"I've sent a parcel of your things with their son, Richard," said Lucy. "He lives not far from you. He is an actor."

There were many actors in Maria's area, along with writers, musicians, and artists. Gabriel and Charlie knew lots of them. There were healers, too, although Maria didn't seem to cross paths with them.

Richard knocked on the door a few days later. Maria couldn't remember him, but when she saw him, she wondered why—a good-looking man about ten years older than her, well dressed in an edgy actor sort of way, polite and quietly confident. He was slightly shy, making him all the more attractive.

"I don't think we have ever met," he said, holding out his hand. "Every time I visit your mother's cafe, she mentions you. I am on my way to get coffee now. Would you like to come?"

"Sure," said Maria. "I'll get my coat. I need a walk."

Maria didn't date. Men sometimes asked her, but she didn't take it up. Although she understood how the dating arrangement worked for other people, she found the idea illogical for her circumstances. Dates, as opposed to catching up with friends, assumed that one was available and interested in some sort of connection, ranging from casual sex to marriage and everything in between. Firstly, Maria didn't feel single. She didn't feel alone. The idea of searching for someone to fill a space didn't make sense to her. Secondly, she could read most people very quickly. The thought of dating a stranger in an awkward, draining, and undetermined situation to find out what sort of person they were (even though it was usually obvious) made her cringe.

Maria and Richard walked to the local cafe, which was buzzing with life. They immediately liked each other and found they had lots to talk about. After that day, they kept in regular contact. As much as Maria liked Richard and enjoyed his company, something about him made her hesitant to get too close. He was not pushing anything. He was too confident for that. He didn't need to ask women for anything. They usually made their intentions more than clear to him.

*That's the problem right there,* thought Maria. *I don't want someone to kiss me, like the man in my dream, and then think about kissing someone else in a year, six months, or six seconds.*

It was a compliment to have Richard's attention. However, a compliment is not enough. It has to feel right. It has to feel…necessary.

It wasn't long before Richard started talking about his new friend. Something in his voice told Maria that this relationship was important to him and was already beginning to change him, as genuine relationships do. Richard said that he would like Maria to meet his new girlfriend. He also said that Maria was the only person he had mentioned it to.

*Why won't he discuss his new relationship with any of his friends and introduce her?* thought Maria. *He is obviously falling in love with her.*

When they all met at the cafe, Maria understood why. She was expecting a woman like Richard, mid to late thirties, good-looking, vibrant, and confident. Richard walked in with his arm protectively around a woman probably fifteen years older than him. She looked good for her age, but Richard looked fantastic and was many years younger. This was not his usual style. Maria was intrigued. The woman was lovely but also strong and independent. No doubt she mothered him, but he didn't seem to mind. Then they would switch. Richard sat her on his lap and kissed her forehead. She laughed and didn't try to escape. He told her that she looked beautiful today. He was probably exaggerating, but no one cared. She did not need to be told she looked beautiful, but took it anyway.

The whole thing was delightful to watch. Maria felt happy for both of them.

*She will give him all the love he needs, and her life experience will make her overlook many of his faults,* thought Maria as she walked home. *But if he starts wandering or lying, she will be on it, sharp and short. She will remind him that he is free to walk out that door. It's precisely the sort of approach Richard needs.*

THAT EVENING, Maria asked Amira, "Am I on the right track to think the way I do, or am I missing the boat?"

"Don't worry about that," said Amira. "It is not for you to decide who you will love and trust. Love those who come into your life. Love them for as long as they wish to be there. And then still love them even if they are no longer there. You cannot run out of love or give too much away. You don't have to decide or arrange anything. Your happiness is already assured."

## CHAPTER 43
## GRACE

Maria had another Waldmeer visitor around the same time that Richard first visited. Mary's mother, Grace, had been ill and needed to see the city specialists. Gabriel was travelling and offered his room to Grace and her husband, Joe, for two weeks. Mary was worried about her mother, and Charlie was worried about Mary. It was a worried household.

Joe was a dairyman, through and through, and he had not been to the city for years. As much as he would do the right thing for his wife, he couldn't wait to get home. He was pacing the house so much that eventually, Mary told him to go back to the cows and that she and Charlie would look after her Mum. Joe was reluctant to agree, but he did. He couldn't help singing as soon as he hit the green pastures on the way home to his four-legged loves.

As Grace wasn't getting any better and the doctors didn't seem to make much difference, Charlie suggested that Grace visit Maria.

"What do you have to lose?" said Charlie.

Not only did Grace visit Maria, but she also told Maria that her house was the only place she felt less pain, so she came every day. When Gabriel returned, it was arranged that Grace would stay in Maria's healing room for the rest of the month and that Maria would have a break from seeing other clients.

Maria asked Amira if she thought letting Grace stay was a good idea.

"Yes, it is," said Amira. "Grace wants to leave, so she has given herself a mysterious illness that will eventually get her that result."

"You mean leave life?" asked Maria.

"Yes," said Amira.

"Why does she want to go?"

"She has been unhappy in her marriage for a long time. She wants to leave her husband, but doesn't want to hurt anyone, and is afraid of the difficulties of such a big change. So instead of leaving Joe, she has decided to leave life, thinking that that will give her some peace."

"Is she conscious of any of this?" asked Maria.

"No," said Amira. "She has never been taught to understand her thinking and feeling processes and finds any self-analysis frightening and disturbing."

"Then we are starting at the beginning," said Maria.

While Grace was in Maria's house, she felt significantly better. However, Maria knew that without Grace's understanding of the underlying issues, her wellness would quickly deteriorate once she left. Each day, Maria suggested information to Grace about the possible thoughts underlying her illness. At first, she had to be very subtle because all Grace would say about Joe was that he was a wonderful man and that she was lucky to have such a great life.

However, healing has its own power and once started, it moves ahead methodically, knowing exactly what track to take for the most efficient and effective results.

One evening, all of Grace's pain returned. Maria used the opening.

"You were just then on the phone with Joe, and he was talking about some of the things that you will need to attend to when you return to the farm," said Maria. "Do you think that your pain could, in any way, be related to your feeling about the farm, Joe, or your life in Waldmeer?"

Grace started crying hysterically.

*Thank goodness,* thought Maria. *She's getting somewhere.*

Maria calmly assured her there was nothing to fear and everything would be fine. Yet, at the same time, she could not miss this window of opportunity because they can be few and far between. Or perhaps it is our willingness to approach them that is few and far between.

"Imagine that your tears could talk," said Maria. "What would they say? Listen to them. They are trying to tell you something important."

Grace cried even more uncontrollably.

"I can't go back," she said. "I would rather die than go back. I feel trapped. I would so dearly love to live a little bit, live my own life, and learn about myself before I die."

"You can, Grace. And there is no need to die," said Maria. "Not for a long time, anyway."

Grace laughed out loud. It was a release. Maria laughed too. She had not seen Grace smile, let alone laugh.

"Perhaps, it would be possible to suggest a little break to Joe, and then you can see how things go," said Maria. "It doesn't have to be a big drama. There doesn't have to be any blame. Even if he gets upset and angry, keep loving him, and he will eventually see that you mean no harm to him, but you must also protect your life path. Your first responsibility is to your own worth. Everything comes from that."

GRACE RETURNED HOME TO JOE, but only briefly. A few weeks later, she rented a little flat on a pretty street near the river in the town closest to Waldmeer. It was a bigger town than Waldmeer, and Grace was delighted with all the opportunities it presented her. Joe was a complaining, bumbling mess when Grace left, but, to everyone's surprise, he pulled himself together after a few months and adjusted to life as a single man. He even asked a local widower out on a date. She was thrilled to have the company of an eligible man. She thought Joe was very handsome and manly. Joe was starting to enjoy life beyond his cows.

As for Grace, she was blessed beyond anything an onlooker could perceive. Even her daughter, Mary, did not really understand the change in her mother. Maria did. She heard it in her voice whenever Grace called. Maria knew the angels were blessing her, and she was becoming close to God. Her little bit of courage was greatly rewarded beyond anything Grace would have expected or even dreamed of. The return of her health was merely the first step.

After a while, Grace and Joe started to catch up for coffee in Grace's new town. Joe would dress up as if he were going on one of his, by now, many dates. They would sit in the cafe and talk about the family, the farm, and Waldmeer. This day, as they parted, Grace reached over and kissed Joe on the cheek. She had much love for him, yet she would never return. Something in the kiss shocked Joe.

"That is the first time you have voluntarily kissed me in ten years," he said quietly, wiping a tear from his eye.

He shuffled his feet and then walked off, saying he would pay the bill.

As they left, Grace turned to him and said, "Thank you for the coffee."

Joe stopped her. "No, Grace, it is I who must thank you."

He again started to cry and quickly turned for the car.

"I'll see you soon," he mumbled.

Straightening his suit jacket and tie, he waved as if he had many important things to attend to.

# MEN

## CHAPTER 44
## HIERARCHY

Maria's dog, Gortaithe, was coming along well. He had relaxed into his inner-city household life, as relaxed as a German shepherd like him gets. He stopped looking aggressively at people and even let them pat him. He wasn't overly enthusiastic about human attention, other than his human, but he tolerated it with relatively good grace. Other dogs, however, were a different matter. Every dog was considered a possible life threat to Maria and treated accordingly. If Maria and Gortaithe walked the streets of Eraldus, he looked like a wild animal pacing the boundaries of his territory—head erect, ears up, leaning forward, eyes peeled. It was hardly pleasant to walk him and disconcerting to other dog owners. Walking the laneways, where dogs didn't tend to go, made life much easier.

It was a calm, bright autumn day with the type of mild, warming sun we crave after a bout of dreary, cold weather. Maria and Gortaithe approached the corner. A huge dog was off-lead and unattended. Maria panicked, expecting an all-out dogfight until she realised it was Galahad from the North Country. Instead of being his usual composed self, he seemed affronted.

"Who is this?" he said, looking at Gortaithe.

Gortaithe, for once, lowered his head, crouched, and backed away. Far from a wild beast, he seemed a boy in the presence of a man. Galahad was still not satisfied. He stared at Gortaithe, who knew to look away.

"Don't cross me," Galahad said to Gortaithe. "Ever."

Then he was gone as quickly as he appeared.

*Well, I'll be,* thought Maria. *Everyone meets their match or, in this case, superior.*

It only took a minute, and Gortaithe returned to his grandly dominant self, strutting the laneways as if he owned the world. Almost.

Ten minutes after returning home, Maria heard a knock at the door.

"Stay," she said to Gortaithe, who knew he had to sit at the far end of the hall although his spirit was bounding for the door.

It was Mr MacArthur. Maria hadn't seen him for years.

## CHAPTER 45
## TIME WARP

M r MacArthur was the school principal of Waldmeer State Secondary School. Maria had known him for her entire schooling. When she was in primary school, he would visit the assembly and give an inspirational talk, which, for that age group, mainly consisted of the request to be kind. He had been the secondary school principal for a hundred years, or it seemed like that to the children. Even their parents couldn't recall when he was not the principal. As with many Waldmeer children, he was the most important father figure in Maria's young life, second only to her father.

"You have greatness inside you. I expect to see it," he would say in the secondary school assemblies.

Then he would add with much gesticulation, "You are not just a small fish in a small pond. You can be a big fish in a big pond."

It was sort of corny, and the students would frequently roll their eyes, but they heard it so many times that it became part of their consciousness in their formative years.

Having had no children of his own, he considered all his students as his children. His wife died about ten years ago. He was highly community-minded and was always winning awards for excellence. He was also always trying to win awards for his students. However, somewhere along the way, he forgot that he had a life apart from school. He seemed to get stuck in a time warp. It wasn't the death of his wife that did it. He felt more comfortable in his work world, where he excelled. He didn't possess the same sense of ease and purpose in the rest of his life. Almost sixty and looking at retirement in the next few years, he had no idea what would be left of him when work finished. For this reason, he started doing a few things that he would never have considered before. They were just little things, but it meant that he had opened something that was previously closed.

On such a whim, he decided to call at Maria's house when he visited the city next. He didn't bother ringing, as he would only go to the door to express his appreciation for Grace's recovery. Grace and Joe's twins, Mary and Harry, had likewise been with Mr MacArthur for their entire schooling. He knew the family well.

"I bumped into Grace recently," said Mr MacArthur when Maria opened the door. "She credits her return of health to you. I wanted to say what a wonderful thing it is that she is well again, and you must be an exceptional person if you can make people well."

Mr MacArthur was the first one to find a reason to congratulate people.

"Oh, how kind of you to call in to say that, Mr MacArthur," said Maria.

"Please call me Thomas," said Mr MacArthur slightly awkwardly.

"We are not at school anymore," he added, trying to sound funny.

It didn't come across as funny, but Maria laughed to break the awkwardness.

"Okay, Thomas," she said with deliberate exaggeration.

She laughed, and Thomas joined in.

"Grace made herself well again," said Maria, "but thank you. I appreciate it."

"I won't keep you any longer," said Thomas. He paused. "I have decided I need a bit of a fashion overhaul, so I am going to the shopping centre now. I'm not good at shopping, and I'll probably buy more of the same clothes I already have, but I'll try."

He said it without his usual enthusiasm in assemblies for inspired living. Maria looked at his clothes. They certainly needed updating. They were very ageing and dreary. She didn't have much hope for his shopping abilities.

As if on cue, Gabriel pulled up and jumped out of the car to drop something off for Maria from Charlie. Maria introduced Gabriel and Thomas. Thomas would be the age of Gabriel's father, who died when he was little. For some reason, they looked at each other a moment longer than usual for strangers. Maria explained Thomas's shopping venture. Gabriel had a natural flair for clothes and enjoyed shopping. He looked at Thomas's clothes and almost screwed his nose up in disdain. Maria tried not to laugh.

"Tell you what," Gabriel said unexpectedly. "I am going to the shopping centre myself. Why don't you follow me, and I'll show you a few good shops."

# CHAPTER 46
# UNLIKELY FRIENDS

When they got to the shopping centre, Gabriel pointed out a few suitable shops to Thomas and said goodbye. Thomas walked up to one of the chosen shops and looked like a fish out of water. Deciding that his old pond was the best option, he headed for the conservative old man's shop next door. He picked up one of the shirts on the rack. He couldn't remember if he had one like it or not. All his clothes looked the same, so it was hard to tell. Gabriel had been watching from a distance. Whether it was disgust or humanitarian aid, he walked over to Thomas and almost grabbed the shirt from his hand.

"It's horrible," he said.

Gabriel walked to the store he had originally suggested, expecting Thomas to follow. He had never been to Waldmeer Secondary School. Gabriel knew his new acquaintance only as Thomas, not Mr MacArthur, and treated him accordingly. Thomas stood blankly for a moment and then obediently followed. He was used to being obeyed, not obeying.

Walking around the shop with a bit of added drama for effect, Gabriel picked out all sorts of clothes for Thomas.

"Try these," said Gabriel, handing Thomas the clothes.

Thomas looked at them and hesitated.

"Look, I have other stuff to do," said Gabriel. "Do you want help or not?"

Then he added with a smile, "I think you need it."

Thomas bought it all, and they both walked out of the shop as if they had won a prize.

"How can I repay you for your help?" asked Thomas.

Feeling that the exchange was not quite finished, Gabriel said, "Buy me a coffee."

As if a barrier had already been broken, they started to talk about things that men don't easily talk about to each other. It was strange that they were so open, being virtual strangers, but many things in life are strange.

"I have decided it is time to get a new lease of life," said Thomas.

"I think I have had a bit too much of a lease of life," said Gabriel.

"What do you mean?" asked Thomas.

"I sometimes wonder if I am wasting my life," said Gabriel. "You have dedicated your life to people and your community. I wonder if I have spent too much of my life thinking about myself."

They seemed like opposites, but, on the other hand, they were alike—good men, well-adjusted, people-oriented, natural leaders, kind-hearted.

"I wish I had your sense of freedom and independence," said Thomas. "It would have saved me from many mistakes."

"What mistakes?" ventured Gabriel.

They had come this far, so Thomas decided to be honest.

"I have spent the last forty years of my life serving others. I do not regret caring about people and have gained many rewards along the way. However, I have also made many choices based on fear. I wish I would have had your courage."

"What sort of choices?" asked Gabriel.

"If I were braver, I would have left my marriage in the earlier years," said Thomas. "But I wasn't, and then the years go on, and it becomes too difficult to change anything. The trouble with staying too long with someone you don't want to be with is that you end up waiting for something to happen that will release you, even sickness or death. And then you feel bad that you could think like that, but what other choice is there when one is a prisoner? You would never let yourself get in that situation."

"No, I wouldn't," said Gabriel. "At least you weren't alone and lonely."

"It was intensely lonely," said Thomas.

"So is freedom," said Gabriel.

"But it's brave," said Thomas.

"Is it?" said Gabriel. "I don't know how brave it is. Maybe it's avoidance. That's not brave."

They both looked at each other, a little lost and forlorn. Being older, Thomas suddenly decided to change tracks.

"You know, Gabriel, I don't think either of us has been wrong," he said cheerfully. "In our ways, we have tried to find happiness. Yet, I don't think either of us is right either."

The waiter took their empty cups and asked if they wanted another coffee.

"No, I have to go," said Gabriel, still sitting there.

"I think there is a depth to life which only comes from our connection to other people," said Thomas. "However, we have to find it without becoming a prisoner. And we must believe that we will be okay no matter what. That gives us courage. I hope it will give me courage, anyway."

Gabriel got up, shook Thomas's hand, and said, "Enjoy your clothes and your journey."

He walked back into the busy shopping centre, but for some reason, he couldn't remember what he had to buy, which was so important a few hours ago.

FROM THEN ON, Thomas didn't buy clothes without Gabriel. He would announce to his secretary that a particular day would be blocked out because he needed to see his stylist. He said the word *stylist* as if no one else would know what it was because he didn't previously know. Thomas and Gabriel became unlikely friends who would help to style each other's lives and thoughts.

# BLISS

## CHAPTER 47
## BLESS

Maria threw her coat on the bed and turned the heater on. The house was cold on her return from the meeting.

"That was a disgrace," she fumed to Amira.

Gortaithe looked sympathetic. He would always be a one-eyed supporter. Amira, however, didn't say anything.

"Conceited, arrogant, egotistical, and delusional," said Maria.

She had been thrilled with the invitation left in her mailbox a week ago.

*You are warmly invited to the first Co-operative Meeting of Eraldus Professional Healers, which the esteemed Bliss Kurt will chair.*

Several semi-famous healers and self-help writers were living in Maria's area. Bliss Kurt was one of them. Tall with long, loose, blonde hair and excellent posture, she was an imposing figure. She had an equally good-looking partner, who Maria later discovered had only been around for the last six months. They looked like a cross between hipsters and movie stars.

Bliss was not precisely what Maria had hoped for, but she told herself that everyone is different. During a break in the meeting, she was in the bathroom when it was empty, except for, fortuitously, Bliss.

*Great,* thought Maria, *I will be able to connect with her when no one else is clamouring for her attention.*

However, Bliss took one look at Maria, acted like no one was there, and started preening in the mirror. After that, she seemed to have made a mental note not to look at Maria, let alone allow her to speak.

It wasn't exactly "a cooperative meeting of Eraldus healers". It was more of a presentation of Bliss's past achievements and future ambitions. Of course, such meetings are full of the words love, peace, and humility. There is an equal abundance of hugging, oming, and namaste-ing with hands prayerfully clasped together. Despite all the *love*, there seemed to be an uneasy feeling of spiritual one-upmanship. There was a lot of name-dropping.

One story that particularly annoyed Maria was Bliss's recollection of socialising with a world-renowned spiritual and self-help leader. "I'm not planning on coming back," he had apparently said to Bliss. He came from an Indian background, and the wheel of reincarnation was an inbuilt part of his view of evolution. "I want this life to be my last," he said. "I think I've done enough to warrant it."

Maria thought that anyone not coming back would not be talking about it. However, this man had done a lot to help humanity, so he was probably entitled to a bit of enlightenment self-promotion.

"I totally agree," Bliss had replied to him, all arms and drama. "I've done soo much to help the world that there is no way I am coming back."

*You've done enough,* thought Maria, *to promote your own pseudo-guruship to last several lifetimes. I am not sure how much you have actually done to help the world.*

The worst thing about the meeting was what Maria witnessed when she decided to quietly leave through the open kitchen door.

"Excuse me, Bliss," said a softly spoken woman in her fifties. "I was wondering if I could join the audience for some of the presentations."

She was wiping her hands on a tea towel after preparing food for the evening.

"Oh, sweetheart," said Bliss patronisingly. "You are coming along so well with your studies, but you are not quite ready to sit with the others. They are professionals, after all. I will let you know when it is time. Continue your service to the Divine, help me with the privileged work without complaint, and the Great One will bless you as it has blessed me."

Bliss then dismissed the woman with her hand as she was very busy. The woman didn't look in the slightest offended.

Maria continued walking through the kitchen. Just outside the door, a man was sitting holding his hand. He had burned himself on the stove. The woman came out to help him. She looked at him with as much love as if he were the world's most precious being.

She took his hand and said, "Edward, dear, don't be upset. There is nothing wrong with you."

The love and peace radiated from her, and Edward decided to jump up.

"You're quite right," he said as if he couldn't remember what the problem was. "I have things to do."

He happily returned to the kitchen, and the woman serenely followed.

*Now, there's a real healer,* thought Maria.

"HEALING IS SIMPLE," said Amira that evening, as Maria complained to her, "if one is healed. The unhealed healer teaches what they live, which is the ego."

"It's my ego that is so annoyed with her, isn't it?" asked Maria. "Bliss is my peer, and instead of showing me respect, she acted like I didn't even exist."

"What else can get offended but the ego?" said Amira. "God is not a professional. Truth is not a profession. The spiritual path is more of an unlearning than a learning."

# CHAPTER 48
# LOVE FIRST, LOVE LAST

"It was a case of hot pants!" said John.

He was one of Maria's clients and didn't want healing. He just wanted to talk, so they decided to stay in the lounge room instead of the healing room. Before he started, he wanted assurance about confidentiality.

"It's a legal requirement," said Maria.

Satisfied, John explained that he was the CEO of a successful business and wanted his personal life to stay personal. He hadn't shared the issue with anyone, including his wife. Particularly his wife.

"As I said, my wife and I married young by today's standards," continued John. "We are only in our mid-forties but have been married for twenty-five years. Mostly, it was too much heat in the pants in our early twenties. Over the years, the passion turned into a respectful partnership, and we are still raising our children. I have been very busy with work and kids, and frankly, I never had much time for interpersonal mumbo-jumbo. I couldn't see the point until I met Sally two years ago. I don't know why, but I adore her. I think about her all the time. She has influenced my life in every possible way. Although I would not like to speak for her, I think she shares at least a little of that feeling for me."

John stared out the window. The climbing roses were creeping along the windowsill.

"I don't know what to do. I have a responsibility to my wife and children. And my marriage is...."

He searched for the word. What was it exactly? If he knew, he probably wouldn't be here.

"Serviceable," he said.

Maria laughed and said, "It serves a purpose."

"Yes, it does," said John, "and I don't want to hurt anyone, but I don't know that I will ever have an opportunity like Sally again. Not to be dramatic, but I feel I can't live without her. She has opened a door for me, and I cannot return to the blind way I seemed to stumble in the darkness before. It all seems somewhat meaningless now."

"Could you speak with your wife about it?" asked Maria. "Or begin the conversation, anyway."

"That might be the end of the marriage," said John.

"Maybe," said Maria. "Maybe not. Are you sleeping with Sally?"

"I know it seems strange," said John, "to love someone that much and not be intimate with them, but no, we are not. I am unwilling to take the risk that it would be the beginning of the end. The relationship is too important to me."

"It's not strange," said Maria, "and it means you haven't had to lie, which saves you a lot of guilt. Guilt is a slow killer. Better to learn how to be more open and let life take its course than live with lies. Lies rob us of our trust, and we project our untrustworthiness onto everyone around us. Have you ever noticed that the innocent are very trusting?

They neither lie nor hold other people's lies against them. Liars, on the other hand, see sabotage everywhere." Maria paused. "Do you love your wife?"

"Yes, I do," John said without hesitation. "Not like I love Sally, but I do. My love for Sally is blissful." He smiled and added, "Maybe, blissfully crazy."

"Well, we do say we *fall* in love," replied Maria. "What can be reasonable or sensible about falling in love? It is crazy, high risk. It is also blissful because we see the divine in the other, and they give the same to us."

Maria stopped to let the divine presence settle into the room. She waited for John to feel the calm, reassuring energy.

"In love relationships," she said, "we become each other's teachers. Do not be afraid of love or the course it will take. There is no certainty in life. Choose love first and choose love last, and it will give you far more than you ever give it."

John stood at the front door and shook Maria's hand warmly.

"I was despairing," he said, "that there could be any right answer. I still don't have the answer, but I have a direction to go."

He looked at the wall hanging behind Maria. It read,

*Except for love, nothing you see will remain.*

# CHANGE

## CHAPTER 49
## LOSS

For the past week, Gortaithe had not been himself. He was restless and jumpy. He kept barking into the empty night even though Maria assured him everything was fine and, when that didn't work, commanded him to be quiet. When they walked in the laneways, he wouldn't relax. He alternated between pulling on the lead and hiding behind Maria. Today was no different. A truck backfired, and he pulled so hard that Maria had to let go of the lead or fall over. Worse, he then ran off.

*What on earth is he doing?* thought Maria.

She ran after him and heard growling and snarling up ahead. The truck backfired again, and then all was quiet.

"Oh my God," she said. "No, no."

Gortaithe was lying in the laneway, soaked in blood, lifeless. Standing over him was Galahad, also streaked with blood. Maria couldn't understand what had happened, but right now, all that mattered was getting help for Gortaithe.

"It's too late," said Galahad. "He has gone."

"No," insisted Maria. "He can't go. It's a mistake. Bring him back. Bring him back."

Gortaithe and Galahad disappeared into thin air. All that remained was the warm blood spread over the cobblestones. Maria ran up and down the laneways calling Gortaithe. Perhaps, she had imagined the whole thing. The laneways were empty. When she got home, she rang the council and lost dog's home in case someone found him. She went into the laneways again. It was getting dark. She had to go home. After closing the curtains, she sat on the lounge and didn't move all night. Sudden loss has a way of immobilising us. Someone was at the door.

*I must have fallen asleep,* she thought with a start.

The doorbell rang again.

*Perhaps, it's news of Gortaithe.*

"Erdo!" said Maria, opening the door.

It was Erdo Kapus from the Leleks. Erdo reached out to Maria and hugged her.

She clung to him and cried, "It's my dog. I'm afraid he has been killed."

Maria first visited Erdo, her mystic teacher, when she was eighteen. She saw him a lot in those first few years, but less so once she moved to the back hills into Charlie's shed. She had not seen him at all in her two years in Eraldus.

"I know," said Erdo. "That is why I have come. Let me come in. I have brought you some food from my garden."

Erdo's food was not just nourishment for the body. It had healing properties. Nevertheless, Maria didn't want it.

"Oh, I can't eat," she said.

Erdo ignored her and walked to the kitchen as if he knew the house well.

"The dear old house hasn't changed much since your

great aunt Rose lived here," said Erdo. "It got a little run down in her later years, but I see you are doing a fine job fixing it up again."

"You knew my great aunt?" Maria asked in surprise.

"Of course," said Erdo. "We all had a crush on her, but she loved us all the same. Once, I almost convinced her to return with me to the Leleks, but in the end, she said it was unnecessary. I tried to tell her I thought it *was* necessary, but Rose was not the sort of woman one contradicts."

Erdo laughed affectionately. Many questions sprang into Maria's mind, but Erdo had busied himself putting the kettle on and placing a vegetable pie in the oven.

"Galahad did not kill Gortaithe," said Erdo. "I know you remember that Galahad warned Gortaithe not to cross him, but that was just a harmless warning."

He pulled out some homemade biscuits from his bag.

"We'll have these with our tea," he said. "It was Rose's sister, Evanora, who killed him. She has been walking up and down the laneways here in Eraldus lately. Gortaithe would have sensed her looming presence."

"Yes, he has been acting strangely for a week," said Maria.

"Gortaithe ran into Evanora in the laneway and lunged at her," said Erdo. "Evanora shot him. Galahad came as quickly as he could, but was not fast enough. Gortaithe died instantly, and Evanora disappeared back into the Shadowland. Because Gortaithe died protecting you, Galahad was allowed to take him back to the North Country."

"Is he in the North Country now," asked Maria excitedly, "with the wolf pack?"

"Yes, he is," said Erdo.

Maria was thrilled.

*He will love it there, and he will be free,* she thought. Another thought crossed her mind. *He can visit me in the laneways as Galahad does. Galahad often brings some of the male pack.*

"No, he cannot come," said Erdo, reading Maria's mind. "He has much training to do. He cannot move between dimensions. It is a learned skill. Also, Gortaithe's pull to this world will be strong for some time yet. If he returned, his attachment to you and his belief in this reality would make it difficult for him to leave this dimension. However, he would not be able to stay here for long. He would end up in the middle of the dimensions, stuck in the dividing line."

Erdo suddenly changed the topic and chatted about his recent forest visitors and students. He then got up and indicated it was time to leave.

Walking to the door, he said, "Gortaithe is not the only one whose path is changing."

## CHAPTER 50
## BIRTHDAY

"I t's me, darling," said the early morning voice on the other end of the phone.

"Hi, Mum," said Maria.

"Happy twenty-sixth birthday," said Lucy. "I was going to post your present, but I also have preserves for you, which are too heavy to post. I made them from the last of our orchard's fruit. I saw Farkas the other day and asked him if he would drop them to you as he is travelling back and forth from Waldmeer, at the moment, for work."

"What sort of work?" asked Maria.

"Oh, who knows," laughed Lucy. "You know Farkas. He is so private. Dad says he could be a drug lord."

"I don't think he is rich enough to be running a drug ring," laughed Maria.

"Well, you never know," said Lucy. "Remember old Mr Perkins in the hills? We all thought he didn't have a cent to his name and often gave him things. Then, when he died, we found out he left a fortune to an estranged relative who also had no idea of his wealth." Lucy laughed at the memory.

"Anyway, Farkas did reluctantly agree. Goodness only knows when he will turn up."

Lucy paused.

"We hope you know how much we love you."

"I do know," said Maria. "And I love you too. I could not have asked for better parents."

A FEW DAYS AGO, *in Waldmeer:*

"I remember when Maria turned eighteen and was working here in the cafe with you," Farkas told Lucy as she handed him the box of preserves and the present.

"Yes, that was eight years ago," said Lucy. "You had not long been in Waldmeer then."

"That long? It seems like yesterday," said Farkas, not wanting time to pass so quickly.

He was now in his late forties. A few more lines, but the same searching eyes. Since his winter in the North Country with the wolf pack a few years ago, he could see and remember more of the other dimensions. However, his recall was still very sporadic and unreliable. Sometimes, he thought he was drunk, and that's why he thought about such things.

## CHAPTER 51
## RELEASE

Maria sat in her lounge room looking into the green, still-overgrown garden. A candle was burning. She watched the flickering light as it unsystematically cast its mystery around the room.

*I wonder how much of Amira is in me by now and how much of Maria remains,* she thought.

One of the flame shadows subtly changed its shape, formed a face, and said, "It has been a long time since I spoke to you in the Homeland, asking if you would be willing to enter Maria's body as the Advisors had asked."

It was Milyaket, Keeper of the Vastandamine Forest.

"I told you that, at first, you would recall Maria's life, experiences, and preferences as if they were your own," she said. "Gradually, you started to hear Amira's voice. That began the transition from Maria to Amira. A slow transition was less stressful for you and your Earth parents. The transition has come to an end. Maria will no longer exist in this domain."

"What does that mean in practical terms?" asked Maria,

for once having a practical thought before any other, perhaps because it sounded like a life and death issue.

"Your questions will be answered more easily in the Homeland," said Milyaket. "We want you to lie your head on the lounge, breathe in slowly, and as you breathe out, we will gently take your soul with us."

THE FOLLOWING MORNING, Farkas pulled up at Maria's house on his way to work. He walked to her door with the box from her mother.

*This box weighs a ton,* he thought. *How many preserves does one woman need?*

Maria's front curtains were open, and he could see her resting. However, she did not stir even after he rang the doorbell numerous times. He put the box down and tentatively walked around the back. The door was not locked, so he walked in. Maria was unconscious but alive. He could not get her to wake up, but she didn't seem in pain or disturbed. She looked quite peaceful. He didn't have any idea what could be wrong and decided the quickest option was to take her to the hospital himself.

At the hospital, Maria was put on a drip and numerous monitors, and Farkas was told to ring her closest relatives. He rang the cafe because that was the only number he had. A stranger answered the phone. When Farkas asked to speak to Lucy, he was told that, sadly, Lucy had died peacefully in her sleep last night. He was also told that his wife's passing had given Lenny such a shock that his heart condition had flared up, and he was now in Waldmeer Intensive Care. The woman asked what Farkas wanted. He told her it was nothing, thanked her for the information, and hung up.

Farkas felt at a loss as to what to do. He left the hospital, telling the nurse he would return later. He put a message in Gabriel and Charlie's letterbox, knowing they would tell people about Maria.

Lenny never did find out about his daughter, not in this dimension anyway.

A FEW DAYS LATER, Farkas remembered leaving Lucy's box on Maria's front step. He drove there and took it inside. He opened the birthday present. It was a cushion that Lucy had embroidered. A note was pinned to it saying,

> *Maria, dear, I found this saying in one of your books that is still on the bookshelf. I'm not exactly sure what it means, but I kept thinking about it, and it almost embroidered itself on the cushion.*

Farkas held the cushion to the light. It read,

> *As you release, so shall you be released.*
> *Forget this not*
> *or Love will be unable to find you.*

He wasn't sure what it meant either, but Maria would know.

"Your mother made you this," he said to Maria when next he visited the hospital.

Maria was silent, of course.

"You will like it," he added.

He put it next to her head. He mostly visited the hospital late at night when no one was around. The night nurses at the desk tried to get him to fill out the visitor's forms, but he always made some joke and kept walking.

"You haven't filled out the visitor's form," a particularly officious, older nurse called to him. "Look here, young man, you must inform me about your relationship with the patient."

Farkas smiled at being called a young man. He continued walking and said over his shoulder, "Write that I am her brother."

# CHAPTER 52
# AMIRA OF ERALDUS

*In the inter-dimensional Homeland:*

Maria arrived in the Homeland bright and happy. That's the thing about the Homeland: once you are there, everywhere else seems miserable. Milyaket explained to Maria about her mother's passing and her father's imminent passing.

"Would you like to help them cross over?" asked Milyaket.

"Of course," said Maria.

"The Advisors have asked you not to speak to them," said Milyaket, "but to transfer your love and calm assurance that all is well. They are both confused by the transition and need time to adjust."

Maria was able to help her mother and, a few weeks later, her father over the bridge into their new state of mind. There was much for them to come to terms with. She silently walked with them, holding their hands—the hands they believed they still possessed—until they were more accustomed to life in the Homeland.

On Maria's last day, Milyaket told her that when she returned to Earth, she would have aged twelve years in terms of biology and demeanour.

"People who already know you will assume it is the result of the mysterious 'illness'," said Milyaket. "With time, they will forget what they thought you were and relate to what you are now."

*That means I will be the same age as Gabriel and Charlie,* thought Maria. *I wonder how they will react to that.*

"As you know, you will return as Amira, your natural self," said Milyaket. "However, like all souls that go to Earth, you will not be in your pure form. Your purity will be substantially dulled by entering Earth's lower base atmosphere. It will be a process of recall."

*IN THE CITY:*

Several weeks after being admitted to the hospital, Amira woke up. It was still dark, but the morning was not far off. There was enough light in the room to work out that she was in a hospital. She pulled out the drip and sat up. Once she adjusted to being vertical, she carefully put her feet on the ground and slowly walked over to the window. She recognised the city landscape below her. Home was not that far away. She left a note on the bed saying she would be back in the afternoon to check out of the hospital properly.

Some of her clothes were in the cupboard. She pulled them on unsteadily and walked hesitantly down the passage, past the desk, and out the glass sliding doors of the hospital. No one stopped her because no one was around. It was wonderful to be outside. Stretching her arms and back, she felt she was coming back to life.

*I'm so hungry that I could eat a horse,* she thought.

That was one of her father's favourite sayings when he returned from being on the fishing trawler.

*I don't know about a horse,* she thought. *Even non-vegetarians probably wouldn't want to eat a horse. This bakery has lights on.*

As she looked through the window, one of the bakers saw her and opened the door.

"Thank you so much," said Amira, taking away a bag of three croissants, a loaf of bread, and a bottle of milk.

She ate all the croissants and drank most of the milk. Now, she could think again. As she travelled on the bus to Eraldus, she tried to make sense of what had happened. How long had it even been? She did not know. She remembered sitting on the lounge in her home and Milyaket visiting. After that, she had no recollection of here on Earth. She did not know how she got to the hospital.

She could recall more of what happened in the Homeland. However, she felt that most of what had been conveyed to her would take a while to resurface in her mind. She did know, very clearly, that Maria was now gone. She knew her parents were safe in the Homeland. She felt no sadness at her recollections. She felt happy as she gazed out the bus window at the city houses with occasional early morning lights. Mothers of little children, shift workers, early risers, restless sleepers, and senior folk who don't need as much sleep anymore.

*I am so blessed,* she thought. *Everyone is so blessed.*

As she stepped off the bus, she realised that sunrise was close. The growing light made the footpaths clear.

"Hi, Maria," said Jack, the paperboy, delivering on his bike. "I haven't seen you for a while. Where have you been?"

He was a boy. No one would have troubled him with whatever had been happening.

"I was having a little holiday, but I'm back now," said Amira.

"Okay, great," said Jack, riding off as if it didn't matter one way or the other.

Fourteen-year-old boys have much more important stuff to think about.

Amira called after him, "By the way, my name is Amira now."

Jack momentarily stopped the bike and said, "My friend's Mum is called Amira. She says it means *one who speaks*. What are you going to say?"

He thought he had made the best joke in the world.

Amira laughed, "Whatever I am told."

# HAPPY MOMENTS

## CHAPTER 53
## THE DANCE

"I'm not calling you 'Amira'," Gabriel said adamantly as they drove to their class. "You already have a perfectly good name."

"Okay," said Amira tolerantly. "It's up to you."

"And also, to be honest," said Gabriel, "I am not enjoying the person you have become in the months since your hospital stay. Frankly, you used to be much nicer."

Amira couldn't help smiling, but she covered it by turning to look out the window.

"I'm just getting older. We get more frank as we age," said Amira. "Perhaps, we are less tolerant of stupidity."

Gabriel didn't laugh at her joke. The only reason he stopped complaining was that they pulled up at the dance class. He was having trouble adjusting to Amira. It was a good sort of trouble. The kind of trouble that makes us grow. The trouble that brings the possibility of fertile, beautiful moments.

This was their fourth dance class. Gabriel had initially seen an advertisement for the class and asked Amira if she would like to go. Like most women, Amira jumped at the opportunity to partner dance. They were having mixed success. It wasn't the dancing—they could both dance—it was other issues.

"You are a *man*, and you can *dance*. That's double points," said Amira realistically. "You will be inundated with dance requests by all the women. You have a right to do whatever you want, but I don't want to dance with other people, and I don't want to sit here by myself. So, if you are not going to dance with me, I won't come."

Gabriel's response was a very reasonable affirmation of his intention to do as Amira asked. He was a reasonable man. However, the requests were mounting each week.

She would remind him, "I'm not coming if you leave me for ages."

"Okay," Gabriel would say, momentarily glancing at her. "I'll try."

*Hmm,* thought Amira. *"Try" is not what I'm looking for.*

However, the dancing would always save the situation. It wasn't all of the dancing. Much of it was spent with Gabriel telling Amira what she was doing wrong. It was the moments, the precious moments. The moments when no one was complaining, blaming, thinking about past hurts, or fearing future ones. It was those moments of simply being present to another person, moments of being grateful. Gratitude for another being, appreciation for life. Those moments made their relationship.

## CHAPTER 54
## HOME

Amira now had a car and could visit Waldmeer every weekend or so. She loved being home so regularly. Besides, there was much to do in caring for another house and garden. She put an ad in the local paper saying that a healer was available once a week in Waldmeer. She made the ad small, hoping conservative folk would not see it. Early on, she felt her parents in the house occasionally.

"Please don't feel you have to visit," she said to them, knowing that they would find a change of dimensions difficult and tiring. "As you can see, I am perfectly fine. I might not look after the house quite like you, Mum, but it's passable, don't you think? You both have other things to think about now. Don't look backwards. Look forwards. Besides, I will soon enough be with you."

Many of Lucy's friends no longer went into Waldmeer Corner Store and Cafe. Amira didn't go in either. One day, while in the other Waldmeer cafe, Amira saw Farkas sitting in the corner, reading the paper.

"Do you mind if I join you for a moment?" said Amira.

"Maria, hello," said Farkas. "How are you? Are you better now?"

"Yes, completely better," said Amira. "I haven't had an opportunity to thank you for taking me to the hospital. I eventually worked out who my 'brother' was."

"The nurse was insistent on knowing who I was," said Farkas, explaining nothing.

He didn't mention that he said he was her brother because Galahad had once told him that Maria was his sister under a different name. Everything about that was confusing, but Galahad was a male of fewer words than Farkas.

"I have a new name now," said Amira. "It's Amira. Do you like it?"

"Amira?" said Farkas. "Yes, yes, I like it. I like it very much. I used to have a friend called Amira."

He struggled to recall who that friend was. It was not only Farkas who couldn't remember his long-ago association with Amira; it was Amira, too. As a human, many things disintegrate when one enters the Earth's atmosphere. Memory is one of them.

"We are closing now," said the waitress.

They walked out of the cafe into the late afternoon. It was the end of winter. They could hear the ocean rolling in, unrelenting and unconcerned with the fast-fading light.

A seriousness grew over Farkas's face.

"I hate winter," he said. "Sometimes, I hate Waldmeer."

He might as well have said, *I hate myself,* but he stopped before those words had a chance to come out. Amira touched his hand.

"Please stop hurting yourself," she said. "That voice you listen to is no friend. It promises so much, but when has it ever given you what it promised? When has it ever given you any happiness longer than a fleeting moment? It has your destruction as its goal, not your happiness."

Farkas put his hands in his jacket. He didn't want to hear such words, but the trouble with words like that is that once heard, they become implanted in our minds. There they grow, whether we like it or not. The road is inevitable for anyone who ventures near it.

"It's not as dark as last week when I was here," said Amira. "The days are getting longer. The cold will be gone soon."

"I'm glad you are better," said Farkas. "I'll go home now."

"Yes," said Amira. "So will I."

## SUMMARY OF WALDMEER SERIES

**The Waldmeer Series**
*A multi-generational journey of spiritual awakening, healing, and the spaces between worlds.*

Beneath the surface of an idyllic coastal village, unseen forces stir. **Waldmeer** is a place where the visible and invisible meet—where inter-dimensional realms brush against everyday life, and where emotional truths rise quietly but undeniably.

Told across **seven books**, the *Waldmeer Series* follows **Maria–Amira** from the groundedness of her rural home to the doorways into higher realms of perception and spiritual transformation. Around her, those she loves and seeks to help are drawn into their own awakenings, resistances, and reckonings.

**Waldmeer moves between ordinary moments and otherworldly initiations. Between earthly love and higher love. Between who we think we are... and what we truly are.**

At times tender, at times confronting, these stories unfold in layers—**personal, relational, and metaphysical.**

This is not a series that looks away from life. It **sees** clearly, **feels** deeply, and **invites** the reader to do the same.

# ABOUT THE AUTHOR

*On the beach at Lorne, Australia (the coastal village Waldmeer is based on).*

Donna Goddard is a spiritual author whose work blends clarity, devotion, and metaphysical insight. With more than twenty published books across spiritual nonfiction, fiction, poetry, and children's literature, she writes to uplift consciousness and offer healing through words.

Donna's Facebook author page has over 400,000 followers from around the world, and her YouTube channel has received more than three million views. Her books are read by spiritual seekers globally and are known for their honesty, poetic style, and transformative energy.

Her writing is an offering—to help others awaken their own inner spirit, trust its guidance, and create a life of depth, beauty, and quiet joy.

All links at https://linktr.ee/donnagoddard

## Ratings and Reviews

Donna would be most grateful for any ratings or reviews.

# ALSO BY DONNA GODDARD

**Fiction**
*Waldmeer Series: A Spiritual Fiction Series*
*Nanima Series: Spiritual Fiction*
*Riverland Series (children's fiction 6 to 9 years)*
*The Fox Tales (children's fiction 8 to 12 years)*

**Nonfiction**
*Love and Devotion Series*
*Spiritual Self Series*
*Dance: A Spiritual Affair*
*Writing: A Spiritual Voice*
*Strange Words: Poems and Prayers*
*Love's Longing*
*Master of Me: Meditations*

Printed in Dunstable, United Kingdom

75443070R00139